ALSO BY
KIMBERLY WILLIS HOLT

Part of Me

KIMBERLY WILLIS HOLT

Stories of a Louisiana Family

SQUARE
FISH

Henry Holt and Company
New York

SQUARE
FISH
An Imprint of Macmillan

Square Fish and the Square Fish logo are trademarks of Macmillan and are used by
Henry Holt and Company under license from Macmillan.

Library of Congress Cataloging-in-Publication Data
Holt, Kimberly Willis.
Part of me : stories of a Louisiana family / Kimberly Willis Holt.
p.   cm.
Summary: Ten stories trace the connections between four generations
of one Louisiana family from 1939 when a young girl leaves school to help support
her family to 2004 when a seventy-nine-year-old woman embarks on a book tour.
ISBN: 978-0-312-58145-9
[1. Family life—Fiction. 2. Louisiana—Fiction.] I. Title.
PZ7.H74023Pa 2006   [Fic]—dc22   2005029676

Originally published in the United States by Henry Holt and Company
Square Fish logo designed by Filomena Tuosto
Designed by Patrick Collins
First Square Fish Edition: 2009
10   9   8   7   6   5   4   3   2   1
www.squarefishbooks.com

For Jerry and Shannon—
you are my home

Part of Me

Family Tree

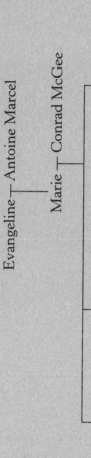

Evangeline ─┬─ Antoine Marcel

Marie ─┬─ Conrad McGee

Vesta Evangeline (Pie)

Luther Harp ─┬─ Rose

Conrad Jr. (Possum)

Merle Henry ─┬─ Lily Bea

Marie

Gordie*

Ryan

Paul Koami ─┬─ Annabeth

Emma

Kyle

*Cecilia, birthmother; raised by Rose

Contents

Rose

Beans and Cornbread

(1939)

PAPA LEFT the summer the windmill broke. Our fields dried up along with Momma's heart and for a while I thought each day was the end of the world. Then the peach tree burst into full bloom and I knew somehow we were going to survive—Momma, Pie, Possum, and me. Momma must have known, too, because she got out of bed one morning and announced, "I t'ink today is a good day for a picnic." So we packed a basket with bread and the last jar of dill pickles, and spread a blanket near the trickle of water that used to be Muddy Creek. That afternoon we listened to the mockingbirds' sweet songs, and when the sun set, the cicadas serenaded us all the way home.

That night in bed, Pie curled under the crook of my arm. "You know what, Rose?"

"What?"

"When Papa comes back, he's going to take me to the World's Fair in New York City. I'm going to ride the Ferris wheel a hundred times and eat cotton candy."

Our little farm outside Amarillo was a long way from New York City. I wondered if Papa was also. I let Pie rattle on and on, though, because she was only nine years old, and because *I* wanted to believe it was true, too.

There was something magical about my little sister. When she was born she came out smiling, dimples and all. Momma named her Vesta Evangeline, but when Papa took one look at her perfectly round face, he said, "You can call her what you want, but she looks just like a pumpkin pie to me." And from that day on she was Pie to all of us. She truly was like dessert—sweet as sugar, but too much of her could give me a bellyache. Sometimes I just didn't feel like being in a good mood and always seeing the sunny side of life.

The only note Papa had left was for me. *Rosebud, fetch Wilbur to fix the windmill.* I guess he feared Momma would let us die of thirst before she asked for help. Wilbur was Papa's former hired hand. That day he fixed the windmill in exchange for some peach preserves.

"I'll do it for nothing, Mrs. McGee," Wilbur had said. "Conrad always did right by me."

Momma straightened her back when he'd mentioned Papa's name. "You take de peaches." It was an order, not an offer.

Wilbur lifted his hat and wiped his forehead with his kerchief before taking the jars from Momma. "I don't know how long that old thing is gonna work."

That's why we stopped watering the fields. Momma wanted to make sure there was enough water for us and the peach tree.

We were the only folks around for miles that had peaches. The story goes Papa had teased Momma when she told him she wanted to plant a peach tree here in the Panhandle. But he drove eighty miles to buy one for her. She babied it like a child, always making sure it had enough water and was covered before a freeze. It had even survived the Dust Bowl. Though we almost didn't. While all the farmers around us took government handouts, to keep from losing their farms, Papa struggled. When it came down to feeding us or letting Wilbur go, Papa begged Momma to let him get some government money. "Today it might be losing Wilbur, tomorrow we could lose the farm."

Momma had folded her arms and narrowed her eyes. "I don't take no charity. And I don't marry no man who take it."

I wondered if that's why Papa left us. Maybe he thought Momma would give up and turn to the government for help.

One August evening we sat at the table eating dinner and heard shuffling coming from the porch. No one admitted they were hoping that the sound was Papa scraping his boots on the mat instead of the wind causing the cottonwood branch to brush against the pillar. But you could see that hope in all of our eyes, even Momma's.

When Papa left, the smokehouse had two hams and a slab of bacon remaining. By late summer, the meat was gone.

We ate beans and cornbread almost every night. And peaches. Thank goodness for the peaches. We'd picked every last fruit off the tree and Momma had filled all the Mason jars we owned with them. Their sweet juice tasted like honey after eating our bland meals.

The only one brave enough to say anything about

it was Pie. "Are we ever going to have meat again?" she asked, twirling a long brown lock with her finger. Momma shot her such a glare that Possum and I left the room to find something to clean.

"If it was cooler, I'd take Radio out and we'd go hunting," Possum said, smoothing down the cowlick he could never tame. "There's nothing but a few measly squirrels around. And they're too bony to be any good." Last winter when he was hunting, Possum rescued a puppy and brought him home. Pie named him Radio because she'd wanted an Emerson radio so bad. We were the only family around that couldn't listen to *The Lone Ranger* and *Little Orphan Annie*.

In September, Pie went to fourth grade, Possum to fifth. I entered my freshman year at the high school, happy because my eighth-grade teacher, Mrs. Pratt, would be teaching me again this year. She liked my stories and I treasured the remarks she made on my papers—*Keep writing. This is outstanding. Your descriptions are lovely.*

Our nearest neighbors lived half a mile away, but word about Papa must have traveled to them. The Saturday before Christmas, the Calvary Baptist

Church Visiting Committee came by with food. We had attended services there with Papa, but Momma was a Catholic from Louisiana and often said, "I worship at home before I do it in a Baptist church."

Once when she said that, Papa had winked at me and whispered, "It was good enough for her to get married in."

Papa teased that he kidnapped a Cajun princess and hauled her all the way to the Texas Panhandle. Those were the kind of moments I tried not to think of—Papa with his little winks and wisecracks that sometimes made even Momma laugh. Mostly they had made her mad. These days anger seemed to be the only thing that could swallow her sadness. Now if she broke a glass, it was Papa's fault. She said his name like a curse until the words "Conrad McGee" faded away and were never heard in our house again. Except for the winter day the Calvary Baptist Church Visiting Committee came calling.

From the kitchen window I watched them walk toward the porch with baskets in their hands. The wind whipped at their skirt hems, exposing their white slips. Skinny Mrs. Ingle wore a red hat while both Miss Thunderwood and Mrs. Cooper wore blue from head to toe. They reminded me of two plump blue jays and a frail cardinal.

"Hello, Rose," Miss Thunderwood said when I opened the door. "My, you're a pretty thing."

Mrs. Ingle centered her hat, which had slid to the right side of her head. "My word, Marie. Is that a peach tree out front?"

"Yes," Momma mumbled.

Mrs. Ingle shook her head in disbelief. "I didn't know peaches would grow up here. My cousin grows them, but he lives all the way over in Hedley."

Momma made them some coffee while they settled at our kitchen table. Possum and I tried not to stare at the baskets of food, even though our mouths watered from the aroma. But Pie just bolted into the room and asked, "What smells so good?"

Miss Thunderwood pinched Pie's cheeks. "Why, honey, we've got biscuits and gravy and fried chicken with corn on the cob." She still had ahold of Pie's cheeks when she added, "You are the spitting image of your daddy."

Pie pulled away from Miss Thunderwood and stepped closer to one of the baskets covered with a gingham cloth. I could see her fingers just itching to dive inside.

Then Miss Thunderwood looked up at Momma. "Where is Conrad anyway?"

"Yes," said Mrs. Cooper, "where is that rascal?"

She took a sip of Momma's strong coffee, then squinted.

Mrs. Ingle chirped up, joining in with the blue jays. "We haven't seen him or the children in months."

Momma's hands flew to her hips. "You bring dis food for my children and me because you t'ink we are starving without Conrad?"

"Oh, goodness no," said Mrs. Thunderwood. "We're just out visiting and—"

Momma picked up the baskets one at a time, and one at a time, handed them back to the ladies of the Visiting Committee from Calvary Baptist Church. They were out the door and driving away from our house in no time. My stomach growled and I thought Pie was going to burst into tears. Possum walked out of the room and I heard him kick the wall. Somehow I felt like everything I'd hoped for went outside the door with those baskets. It was only food, I kept trying to convince myself. But it was as if my dreams of becoming a writer were tucked between the biscuits and the fried chicken.

That night I slipped my sweater over my night-gown and stepped onto the porch. I needed the cool air, but most of all I needed to get away from Momma. I collapsed onto the porch swing and rocked back and forth on the balls of my feet. The sky was black and the stars covered it like sugar sprinkled across a cookie. I was thankful that I couldn't look out and see the dry fields that made me think of Papa and how hard he'd worked trying to keep them watered. And I was glad that I couldn't make out the road leading up to our house. Many days I stared at it so long that I could almost imagine Papa walking toward us, smiling like he was about to burst with the best news in the world.

Straightening my legs, I held the swing back for a moment. Then I heard something hit the wood floor.

It was too dark to see so I patted the floor, searching until I felt two books and an envelope. Maybe the church ladies dropped them accidentally. I took off my sweater and wrapped the items with it before going inside the house.

Momma was already in bed, but Possum and Pie were playing cards on the floor next to a kerosene lamp. I lighted the other one and headed toward the outhouse, not wanting anyone to discover me. Inside I hung the lamp on the nail and uncovered the books. The envelope said "Rose" across it. One of the books was *The Good Earth* by Pearl S. Buck. The other was a brown leather book.

I tore the envelope and read the letter.

Dear Rose,

*The women from the church visiting
committee said they would be happy to
give these books to you when they went
calling. You are a gifted student and
writer. Always keep the words flowing
from your pen.*

Sincerely,
Mary Pratt

I opened the leather book and discovered it was
blank. Every single page was just waiting for words.

The beans ran out the day after Christmas. Momma
didn't say anything, but that afternoon she gave us
each a box to squeeze our belongings in. We were
given strict orders to take only what could fit in the
box. And I was surprised when Momma softened
and let Radio come along.

After we finished packing the truck, I slipped in
beside Momma, while Pie and Possum rode in the
back with Radio. A second later, Momma started

the engine and headed east toward her birthplace in south Louisiana.

I didn't look back. I didn't want to see our little farmhouse disappear from sight, fearful that it might disappear from my memory forever.

There hadn't been enough money in the flour tin to stay at a hotel, so every night, Momma pulled off the road and we slept in the bed of the pickup. That first evening on our journey, I ignored Pie while she asked Momma a million questions. But I listened for Momma's answer when she asked, "What does Houma look like?"

Momma grabbed Pie's hand and held it up in the moonlight. She traced the space between her fingers. "Deese are de bayous. De rest is de land." She touched the valley between two of her fingers. "I grew up here next to Bayou du Large."

Pie thought she was on an adventure. But she had the sense of an old dumb cow, standing in the middle of the road, chewing its cud while cars moved toward it. Except for Papa leaving, Pie hardly knew a bad time. Everything was fun to her.

Momma had been driving for two long days and she'd grown tired of it. Most of the way, I'd ridden on the passenger's side, sometimes trading spots with Possum or Pie, who seemed to like sitting in the back of the pickup.

The third morning Momma pulled over to the side of the road and stopped the engine. "All right, Rose. Time for you to drive."

"But I don't know how to drive," I told her.

"And how you going to learn?" Momma tightened her lips and glared at me.

There was no arguing with her. When she got out, I slid over into her place behind the steering wheel. She didn't give me any instructions. No "put the key in the ignition and turn it." No "put your foot on the brake." No "push in the clutch." Not Momma. She leaned her head against the window and said, "Drive, Rose." Then she quickly fell asleep.

I froze and looked into the rearview mirror at my little brother and sister, who looked like their eyes were going to pop out of their sockets. I wanted to nudge Momma and wake her and ask, *What do I do?* But she probably would have said, "I drive for hundreds of miles and you don't know what I do?"

My hands were sweaty. I wiped them on my skirt and turned the key. The engine started, but I got the brake mixed up with the clutch. The truck jerked forward and back. Then it took off down the side of the road. I stuck my head out the window and hollered back, "Hang on!"

Even though it was a bit bumpy, the grass seemed a safer place to be. I would have continued on that way, but Momma opened her eyes.

Without moving, she said, "Get on de road." Then she shut her eyes again.

Momma slept as I sweated and hoped that no one would pass us on the road. And when a black car got close behind us, I held my breath and swerved to the right. Pie, Possum, and Radio juggled to and fro in the back of the pickup like three marbles being shaken in a jar.

The next morning, Momma handed me the key. "You gonna drive today."

Possum and Pie yelled, "NO!"

Momma sighed and got back behind the steering wheel. She never asked me to drive again, because that day we crossed the state line into Louisiana. "If we don't watch out," she'd said, "we'll get pulled over with deese Texas plates."

The day before we reached Houma, Possum rode in the front with Momma while I sat in the back with Pie. It was warm even though it was December. We passed bare sugarcane fields that had recently been harvested. Stalks that had dropped from the trucks littered the road. Maybe Papa would have stayed if he'd had a Louisiana farm where rain fell almost every day. In the last hour, gray hills and valleys had formed in the sky. I dug out Papa's rain slicker from behind the boxes and unfolded it.

Pie glanced down at Papa's slicker. I knew she was thinking of him. "How will Papa know we're in Houma?"

I swallowed a lump that had formed in my throat. "He left us, Pie."

"But he'll go back to the farm and he won't know where to find us."

Pulling her close to me, I said, "He's not coming back." I knew it now, just as sure as I knew there wasn't a man on the moon.

Fisherman

(1939)

MOMMA MIGHT AS WELL have flown us to the moon. Because Houma looked nothing like Texas. Land seemed to be an afterthought in Houma with slivers of it squeezed between the dark bayous. When I asked, "How does anyone farm out here?" Momma said, "Dey don't. Dey fish."

Moments after we arrived in Houma, we were looking into the face of an old man that we'd been told all our lives was dead. It was like staring at a ghost. Our grandfather, Antoine Marcel, studied us like we weren't from this world either. Momma hadn't bothered to stay in touch with him since she left eighteen years ago, and he knew nothing of us.

We stood, facing him, soldiers ready for inspection.

Even Radio sat at attention. The way Antoine Marcel's stare traveled from our heads to our toes, I half expected him to check behind our ears for dirt.

He rubbed his white beard and studied Momma's face. "You look old," he told her.

"You look older," she told him.

"I think you look like a skinny Santa Claus," said Pie. She smiled at him so big her dimples appeared. I hated Antoine Marcel for giving her nothing back but a frown.

Glancing from him to Momma, it seemed like we were watching a standoff in front of a saloon. Instead we stood in front of his home, which was perched upon tall stilts and squeezed on a narrow strip of land along Bayou du Large. His neighbors' homes were close by, built high off the ground, too. Momma said they were built that way to keep the water from coming into their houses when the tide rose too high, especially during a hurricane. We'd waited out tornadoes in our storm shelter before, but I'd never been in a hurricane. Judging by the height of those stilts, the water must sometimes rise as much as twenty feet.

Docked by the homes were fishing boats with women's names painted on them—*Irene, Josephine, Betty*. Standing there with the salty breeze blowing through my hair, I longed for our white farmhouse with its wraparound porch overlooking the land that stretched to the horizon. *Why did you bring us here, Momma?*

That first night in Houma we tried to be as quiet as mice, tried to take up as little space as possible. The sofa became Possum's bed, and I slept with Momma and Pie in Momma's old bedroom. We hadn't eaten since our breakfast of Rice Krispies, straight from the box. But we didn't ask for food. Surprisingly, Pie didn't either.

Antoine Marcel acted like we were invisible. He ate his breakfast of eggs, grits, and toast alone, not offering us a crumb. Momma waited until he left to gather his oysters before she slipped into the kitchen to get us a bowl of rice for breakfast.

Pie studied her bowl. "I bet Chinese people eat rice for breakfast, too."

"Rose," Momma said, "you take Pie and Possum to school today. I need to find some work."

"Shouldn't I go to the high school after I take them?"

"Tomorrow," she said, looking past my shoulder, avoiding my eyes.

She made sandwiches for the three of us, spreading a thin layer of blackberry jelly on crusty slices of

French bread. I didn't know why she was so stingy with the jelly since there were three full jars of it. It was as if she didn't want to owe Antoine Marcel anything more than she already did.

Before beginning her job hunt, she dropped us off at the grade school. In the office, I filled out paperwork for my brother and sister. The women studied us suspiciously.

"Where are you from?" the school secretary asked. She was shaped like a bell, skinny on top and a big round rear. I swear she'd ring if she wiggled.

"We're from outside Amarillo," I told her.

Every woman in the office looked up at us.

"And why did you move here?"

I didn't know how to answer that. I wasn't going to say because our papa left us and we had nowhere else to go. So I said, "We're staying with my grandfather for a while." It was the plain truth.

The school secretary's eyebrows shot up. "And who is your grandfather?"

"Antoine Marcel."

She looked like I'd socked her right between the eyes. "Antoine Marcel? The oyster man? I didn't know he had any grandchildren. Is Marie your mother?"

"Yes."

"And Conrad McGee is our papa," Pie said.

I hadn't heard the mention of Papa's birth name in so long.

After filling out the forms, I headed back to Antoine Marcel's house, hoping I wouldn't have to go through the same nosy questions tomorrow when I started school.

At home, I wrote in my journal. I wrote more than I'd ever written before. I wrote about the journey, Momma's lie, this new place, this new grandfather—the oyster man.

Momma got a job that day, working as an oyster shucker at the Boudreaux Oyster Company. She came home that first night looking like she'd hitched a ride in a tornado. Some of her dark hair had escaped the pins, and her dress was wrinkled like it had never been in contact with an iron. Scrapes and cuts covered her hands and forearms. Her face looked pinched, and instead of smelling like the Emeraude perfume, she smelled like bayou.

That evening, Antoine Marcel fried a huge platter of oysters, too many for him to eat. The smell of the hot oil cooking those oysters drove me crazy. He slathered some bread with mayonnaise and ketchup.

Then he placed some oysters on top, shook some hot sauce over it, and ate at the table alone, again. After he washed his dish, he pointed to the heap of oysters. "Someone better get rid of dose oysters. Dey won't be no good tomorrow. Maybe dat dog of yours will want dem."

We wanted them, but we waited until he left the room, then hurried toward the platter like hungry orphans. I'd never tried an oyster and if I hadn't been so hungry I would have spit out the salty, squishy thing. Momma must have noticed my disgust as I struggled to swallow because she said, "Deese oysters fed and clothed me."

Momma said that every Tuesday and Friday afternoon Antoine got into his pirogue and rode up and down the bayous playing his fiddle, letting folks know that he was there with his oysters. She said, "All along de water, people call out, 'Antoine Marcel is coming!' And dey meet him on de docks with sacks in der hands."

"How does he steer the boat and play the fiddle at the same time?" Possum asked.

"I used to steer de boat," Momma said. "I don't know who does now." She stared at the wall, and I could tell her mind was a million miles away.

"These oysters taste funny," Pie said, then she seemed to notice Momma's frown and quickly added, "but I think I like them."

"They're delicious," Possum said, gobbling down a half dozen in no time at all. But he thought possums and squirrels tasted good.

After we finished eating, we went outside and fed some to Radio, who ate them right up, then sniffed and licked our fingers.

"How was school?" Momma asked my brother and sister.

"My teacher talks funny, just like you, Momma," Pie said.

For the first time in a very long time, Momma laughed. "Don't tell her dat."

"Oh." Pie sucked in her lips, and of course, we all knew she already had.

That afternoon I had waited for my brother and sister outside the school building. Pie came out of the main entrance skipping, her long hair bouncing with each step. She chattered away, covering every minute of her day in detail. Possum hadn't said a word.

Now Pie was telling it all again. I escaped into the bedroom and read chapter four of *The Good Earth*.

I wondered what books we would read in my new English class. Rain began to fall, hitting the roof with a loud patter. I was deep into the story when Momma handed a newspaper to me.

"Read dat," she said, pointing to a classified ad. Her Cajun accent had grown even stronger since our short time in Houma.

WANTED: BOOKMOBILE DRIVER
Must be 17 with a chauffeur license
Must know how to read
Contact the Terrebone Parish Library

"I'm fourteen," I said.

"You look seventeen."

"That's lying."

"Dat's surviving. You want to stay with dis old grump forever? We need to make money so we can move into our own place. You go back to school later."

My heart plunged. "When?" I asked.

"Not long. A year." Momma picked up an old copy of *Ladies' Home Journal* she'd brought with her from Texas and flipped to one of the stories.

A year was a long time. And how could I trust her about going back to school then? She'd lied about my grandfather being dead. Momma thumbed through the magazine while I listened to the pulse of the thunder as lightning flashed outside the window.

Momma was becoming someone I didn't know. I missed Papa. I missed his easygoing manner, his hearty laugh that ended with a high pitch. We needed Papa here to balance out Momma and her crazy ideas.

That night I opened my journal and wrote.

My dream of becoming a writer is like a fallen leaf swept up by the wind—dancing inches from my reach, teasing, never letting me touch it. But somehow I hope that my life will have some meaning one day.

The next morning, I sat at the courthouse, saying my new birth year over and over in my head. *1922. 1922.* I was thankful that I'd brought my book to read, because no one seemed to be in a hurry to give me a driving test. A woman wearing a blue suit told me to sit on a bench in the main hallway outside the office and wait until they could help me. Then she disappeared into the office directly across the hall.

Try as I may, it was hard not to be distracted. Thick Cajun accents flowed from the offices and I tried to understand what they were saying. When I wasn't carried away by their voices, I was consumed with thoughts of how I would ever pass a driving test when I'd driven only one day in my life.

I wished I'd driven more on the way to Houma. I probably didn't stand a chance to get that bookmobile job. Now I wanted it more than ever, because I knew I'd have to work, no matter what. I didn't want to stand morning until night like Momma. At least Momma hadn't dragged me to the Boudreaux Oyster Company to work beside her.

When the clock struck noon the people in the courthouse poured out of their offices and left for lunch. "You'll have to go, miss," the woman in the blue suit said. "We're closing for lunch."

"But I didn't have my driving test yet."

"Come back at one o'clock," she said, unsnapping her purse to fetch her lipstick.

Bayou du Large was too far to walk back for lunch. Momma had dropped me off that morning on the way to work. Later I was to walk to the Oyster Company and wait for her to finish working. Then we'd ride home together.

I left the courthouse and walked around the town. An aroma of gumbo and fried fish drifted from a diner. My stomach grumbled, but I didn't have any money. So I strolled down the street, peering into the store windows.

In a barbershop, I noticed a handsome man with sandy hair, holding a toddler on his lap. The barber moved around him with his long, narrow scissors, trying to cut the boy's hair. The little fellow scrunched up his face, poked out his lips, and began to wail. His father looked helpless, bouncing the child on his lap. Finally the poor barber threw up his arms, surrendering.

When the boy turned my way I smiled and gave him a small wave. His face relaxed and his blue eyes lit up. He smiled, pointing at me with a plump finger. His father looked in my direction with the same blue eyes and when he noticed me, he grinned. Now the barber was smiling at me, too.

I hurried away, embarrassed. I wasn't used to men smiling at me, just boys back in Texas. Only every time they gazed at me, with that longing-for-a-kiss look, they made me think of how they could stop my future plans cold. Now Momma had done that for me.

"Rose!" The voice came from behind.

I swung around and discovered Antoine Marcel standing outside the barbershop. He started toward me and I waited for him to catch up.

"Rose, what you doing looking in barbershop windows smiling at men for?" The two vertical lines between his brows deepened.

I felt like he'd knocked the breath right out of me. "I was just walking by the barbershop and I only smiled at the little boy."

"I just learn about you. Now you gonna make me disclaim you?"

Something surged inside me. "Isn't that what you did to Momma?"

Antoine Marcel lowered his eyebrows. "Why you talk like dat? Your momma is de one who left me."

I stared down at my book. I knew better than to sass my elders, but I didn't feel much like apologizing.

"What you doing down here?" he asked.

"I'm trying to get my chauffeur's license."

He twisted up his face. "Chauffeur's license? You going to drive a bus?"

"I'm applying for the bookmobile driver's position at the library."

"Dat new library?"

"I think it's new."

"How old are you?"

"Four—seventeen. I'm seventeen."

His eyes narrowed. "What year?"

"Nineteen twenty-two," I said without hesitating.

"Nineteen twenty-two?" His chest rose and fell as he stared at me in a trance. "I thought so."

I wondered what he meant by that, but I didn't ask. "No one will pay attention to me at the courthouse. I've been waiting all morning and now everyone's at lunch."

He rubbed his beard. "You need patience to catch de fish."

"I'm not a fisherman."

"You live here, you better learn to be a fisherman. Don't dat Texan teach you to fish?"

"You mean Papa? He taught Possum."

"I see."

"I have to go." I turned on my heel and hurried away. I didn't like how Antoine Marcel called Papa "that Texan." He said it as if Papa wasn't worth the ground he walked on.

At one o'clock, I reached the courthouse, but the doors were still locked. Finally, at 1:15, a few people returned, including the woman in the blue suit. I found my place back on the bench in the hall and sat.

Twenty minutes later the woman came out of the office and said, "What is your name, miss?"

I straightened. "Rose McGee."

"McGee. Hmm, don't know any McGees." She seemed to be waiting for me to explain. When I said nothing, she went back inside the office and turned on the radio. "The Music Goes Round and Round" played.

I guess McGee was the wrong name for Houma. It didn't sound like Arceneaux or Lirette or Dupre. Maybe I should try to talk like Momma. Then they'd at least think I belonged here. The last few years, I'd gotten pretty good at imitating Momma's accent. It made Papa laugh. Of course, I never let her hear me.

People came and went in the next hour. No one else was asked to sit on the bench and wait. They seemed to get what they came for and then they left. The afternoon sun streamed into the hallway through the glass panels making it difficult to read. I looked at the clock: *2:30*. I was midway through chapter ten. I closed the book and sighed. I tapped my foot. I chewed my thumbnail. Why were they ignoring me? Was it because they'd never seen me before? Then I realized that even if I got their attention and they gave me the test, I'd probably fail.

The main entrance door opened, and I saw the outline of a man walking in my direction. The sun's glare made the hallway bright. Purple dots floated in front of my eyes as I tried to see the man's features. By the time I realized the man was my grandfather, he'd passed me by and disappeared into the office. I've been waiting as patient as a fisherman, I wanted to tell him. And see, it's no use.

A second later, I heard the woman's voice. "Well, Antoine. Look, everyone—it's Antoine Marcel." There was such a commotion you would have thought President Roosevelt had walked inside their office.

A man said, "Hey, Antoine, you brought us some oysters?"

"If you like," my grandfather answered, "I get you some. First I want you to meet somebody."

Suddenly four people—my grandfather, the woman, and two men—were in the hallway in front of me.

"Dis is my granddaughter, Rose."

"Dis is your granddaughter?" the woman asked.

"Dat's right."

"Oh, she's a pretty t'ing," said a man with suspenders traveling over his barrel belly.

"You must be so proud." The woman smiled at me like she was seeing me for the first time.

Another man scratched the dome of his head. "What she doing here?"

I started to say something, but everyone's attention was directed toward Antoine Marcel.

"She needs a chauffeur license," my grandfather said.

"A chauffeur license?" the heavy man asked. "A pretty little t'ing like her? What she gonna do? Drive de bus?"

Everyone laughed, except me.

"Dat's what I say, Thomas. But no, she wants dat job at the library." They were closing in around my grandfather. He stood in the center of their circle, nodding, his arms and hands flying about as he spoke.

"Ooooh, dat's a nice library," Thomas said. "Dey got all kinds of books der."

The woman nodded. "Yeah, my aunt was one of da women dat got dat library going."

"Dat something, all right," said Antoine.

"What she gonna do at dat library?" the woman asked.

No one was bothering to ask me. My blood boiled under my skin.

"She want to drive dat bookmobile," Antoine said. Then they all talked at once.

"How nice." "I see." "Oh. Dat right?"

Antoine nodded. "Dat de truth."

Thomas tucked his thumbs under his suspenders and leaned against the wall. "Well, why didn't you say so?" He was looking at me. Now everyone was looking at me.

Then Thomas turned toward the woman and said, "Give dat girl her chauffeur's license."

He turned toward my grandfather. "Antoine, it was good to see you. I'll be looking for dos oysters." Thomas walked back into his office and Antoine tipped his hat to me before leaving the courthouse.

The woman motioned me inside the office. Finally I was going to get a chance at that driving test. A tremble shook through my whole body. My mind tried to trace that one day I'd driven in Texas. I wondered what kind of vehicle I'd have to drive to get a chauffeur's license. Would I remember how to shift? Would they make me drive on a busy road?

"My name is Jeanette," the woman said. "So your momma is Marie?"

"Yes, ma'am."

"She broke your grandpa's heart when she ran away."

I bit my tongue to keep from saying something that might stop me from getting that license.

Jeanette took my picture and slid a paper across the desk.

Filling out the form, I was careful to write 1922 as my birth year instead of 1925.

Jeanette flicked her eyes over the page when I gave it back to her. "Nineteen twenty-two? I t'ink dat was de year dat Texan came and took your momma away." She peered over the paper.

I felt myself blush, realizing what she thought she was putting together. My face grew hotter when I recalled the conversation Antoine and I had earlier. Momma never was good at math. She should have thought about what people would think they were putting together about her and Papa by making me three years older.

"Sign here," Jeanette said, handing the form back to me.

Ten minutes later I walked out of the office with my chauffeur's license without a driving test.

Outside the courthouse, Antoine Marcel was leaning against an oak tree, his arms folded across his chest. "See," he said, "what I tell you? You need to be a fisherman."

Books on the Bayous

(1940)

MOMMA'S WORKDAY was longer than mine, so I dropped her off each morning at the Boudreaux Oyster Company, before heading to the library. My first day on the job I was paired with a librarian who had just graduated from Louisiana State University in Baton Rouge. Marlene Dupre was pretty with long black hair, eyes dark as coal, and a pug nose that looked like it belonged on a child's face. She grew up in Houma, on Bayou Blue, and knew everyone there and everything about them. She talked nonstop, her arms moving at the same speed as her lips. Sometimes I had to duck to dodge her hands.

The best part of the morning was at the library, choosing the books to load onto the bookmobile.

The librarians picked most of the titles, but they let me make some choices, too. I included books I'd read and loved and books I planned to read.

Marlene chose books while she chatted about her sister Irene's trip to New Orleans and about her zillion uncles. I was amazed at how she could select books while talking about something entirely different. "Now my uncle Rene, he likes tall skinny women. He's the only man in Little Caillou that I know that—" She stopped and held up a book. "Oh, this is a good one. A young girl in love makes the wrong decision and leaves her true love, they get another chance, but in the end they never get together." Well, that just plain ruined the story for me.

The bookmobile was a truck that had been converted to include outside shelves. They held 360 books. We placed the adult books on the right, books for the children and high school students on the left. After we loaded the bookmobile, we lowered the doors that covered each side like shades slipping down a window. Then we latched them. I got in the driver's seat and silently prayed to Saint Jude, patron of hopeless cases. For that's how I surely saw myself behind a steering wheel. At first I thought I had an instant answer to my prayer because the engine started purring. But then I couldn't remember what to do next.

Marlene winked at me. "Come on, baby. It's time to go."

I shifted and we were off with a jerky start, moving down the road like a prancing rooster, thrusting its neck back and forth.

Marlene braced herself, holding on to the dashboard. "Is something wrong with the bookmobile? It's brand-new. What do you think could be wrong?"

She kept shooting out questions and I kept ignoring them, trying to find the right gear to ease us into a smooth rhythm. My heart beat fast.

Finally Marlene grew quiet. I glanced over at her. She held her stomach and her face took on a pale shade of green. "Stop, please!" she cried.

I swerved to the side of the road and braked.

Marlene opened her door, leaned way over, gripping the handle, and vomited.

I felt awful. I dug inside my purse and found a handkerchief. Offering it to her, I said, "I'm so sorry."

After she cleaned herself up and reapplied her lipstick, she asked, "Baby, you do know how to drive, don't you?"

"Yes," I said. "I've just never driven a bookmobile before."

We jiggled along as I desperately moved the stick shift. Maybe St. Jude thought I'd suffered enough because a minute later I found the right gear. After that, something clicked with my head, my hands, and my feet, and it was as if I'd been driving all my life. Then the only bumps we felt were caused by potholes in the dirt roads.

Marlene recovered quickly and said, "Let's start at the school in Bayou du Large, then head on to Little Caillou."

As worn out as I was from Marlene's talking, I was grateful she was with me, serving as my compass.

At the school in Bayou du Large, Possum acted as if he didn't know me, checking out a book quickly, then racing back inside the building. But Pie jumped off the seesaw and came running, then clung to my waist.

"This is my big sister," she told her teacher and the other children.

I was embarrassed because I was supposed to be working and it was hard to work with a nine-year-old attached. No matter how I tried, I couldn't shake her off. Then I looked down at my little sister, smiling up at me, and a warmth spread through my body.

Pie thought I was special because I drove a book-mobile. She wasn't shamed by the fact that I was a high school dropout. I hugged her.

"Tighter," she said.

I squeezed her, this time breathing in her sweaty playground smell. Finally she released her hold on me, satisfied.

The children were so excited about the books. Pie chose *The Hidden Staircase*, a Nancy Drew mystery, then gave me a quick hug before returning to the school with her classmates. Watching them leave with books in their hands made me feel like I was part of something important.

In Montegut, we waited twenty minutes before anyone came. We thought about leaving, but then I saw the handsome man from the barbershop pushing his little boy in a wooden wheelbarrow toward the bookmobile. The man's shirt was wrinkled like he'd put it on straight from the clothesline. I hated ironing, but suddenly a vision of me, pressing every crease out of his shirt, flashed in my mind.

"It's Luther Harp," whispered Marlene. And those words came out of her mouth as light as a feather.

I tried them on for size. "Luther Harp," I whispered just as he reached us.

"Hello, Luther," Marlene said. "Hey there, little Gordie."

Marlene offered Gordie a lollipop we'd bought at the store when we stopped for lunch. Gordie's chubby fingers let go of the wheelbarrow and aimed toward the candy.

"How's Cecilia?" Marlene asked.

"Doing poorly," Luther said, studying me. I guess he thought he recognized me, but I didn't want to remind him that I was the girl gawking through the barbershop window. He picked up *Riders of the Purple Sage*, then he asked, "Anything here for Gordie?"

I quickly grabbed *Mike Mulligan and His Steam Shovel*. "He might like this one."

Luther took the book from me, holding his gaze a little too long. "Thank you."

My face grew warm. Luther Harp was the prettiest man I'd ever seen.

"This is Rose McGee," Marlene told him. "Her grandpa is Antoine Marcel."

"The oyster man?"

"Yes," I said. For once, I was grateful for my grandfather's familiar connection with people.

"She just moved here from Amarillo."

"Texas, huh?" Luther nodded like that explained everything.

"Luther's not from here either. He's from up around Alexandria."

"Forest Hill," Luther said. "Thanks for the books." He put them in the wheelbarrow with Gordie, then picked up the handles and ran along the side of the road.

"Wheee!" Gordie cried as they raced away. Luther's long body moved with grace and ease.

We watched them awhile, then Marlene seemed to awake from her daze and hollered, "Wait, Luther. We need to check out the books first."

That's the way it had been all day. People in Houma weren't used to a library or a bookmobile. "We have to teach them the process," Marlene said, like it was the most important mission on this earth.

As we left Montegut, Marlene explained, "Luther's wife is real sick. She has been for a month. Thank goodness her people live here, or he'd have to stop fishing to take care of their baby. It's the most pitiful thing."

"How old is she?" I asked.

"Cecilia is about my age, twenty-one. I think Luther is twenty-five."

*   *   *

The narrow road to our last stop, Pointe-Aux-Chenes, traveled between skinny strips of land bordering the water. It seemed like the end of the world. And when I told Marlene that, she laughed and said, "Oh, baby, it is. When it rains hard, children here don't go to school because they can't get there. The water hides the road and blends into the bay. My uncle Thomas is a teacher and he says their families take them out of school during trapping season. They miss so much school, it's hard for them to catch up."

"That doesn't seem fair." I said it for them and me.

"Baby, they've got to eat."

We parked across from the general store and waited twenty minutes. A few people passed by us on the way to the general store and gave the bookmobile a long looking-over, but they didn't stop.

Marlene sighed. "They just don't know what to think of us."

Then she said, "You stay here. I'll be right back." She hurried across the road and went inside the general store, letting the screen door slam behind her. Two minutes later, she came out with a woman wearing a blue scarf tied around her head, and carrying a bag of groceries in her arms. Marlene was walking and talking fast, and her arms moved like they were propelling her across the street. The woman glanced around, following reluctantly. I knew right as rain that Marlene had recruited her to be the first person in Pointe-Aux-Chenes to check a book out of our bookmobile.

Marlene appeared so proud of her catch. "This is Julia."

Julia stared at the ground.

"Hi," I said.

The woman peered up at me, shyly. She looked to the right and then to the left like she was planning an escape route.

"She's Antoine Marcel's granddaughter," Marlene said, as if she was introducing her to a royal duchess.

Julia nodded, her lips forming a small smile. "He's got dem good oysters."

I walked to the adult side and selected *The Good Earth*. I would never forget those characters or the story. I held out the book to her.

Marlene seemed taken aback and shook her head. "Oh, I don't know if she'd like that one."

Julia took the book from me. "I'll try dis."

"Why, of course," said Marlene. "Of course you can read that."

But when we drove away, Marlene said, "I don't think she can read that book. I don't think she's had much schooling."

My face burned like a furnace. Suddenly my good deed seemed foolish.

Marlene smiled and said, "You never know, though."

I wondered what Marlene would think if she knew I hadn't finished school either. But Marlene just jabbered away about a movie she'd seen last weekend. "Have you seen it?" she asked me. "Well, it was good all the way until the ending. And then the main character just up and died."

Back at the library, we unloaded the books and shelved them. Then I drove over to the Boudreaux Oyster Company to pick up Momma. I waited in the truck, watching people leave. Most were women. Even though their faces were young, they walked out looking old. Their shoulders slumped and their heads looked at the ground like they were searching for a lost coin.

Twenty minutes later, I decided to go inside to find Momma, thinking that she'd just forgotten the time. I passed the hills of empty oyster shells piled outside and opened the heavy door to the factory.

A clacking noise filled the building, and there was an overwhelming salty smell of the sea. Momma stood behind a long table with eight other women. They each held knives, opening the shells to their own rhythm.

"Momma," I said.

She looked up, slowed her pace a bit, and shook her head. A deep line had etched its way across her forehead. "I can't go home. We got a big order to fill."

"Do you want me to pick you up later?"

"No. I get a ride. Go home." She swept at the air as if to push me away quickly.

I left, walking back to the truck, thinking how Momma really had been looking out for me. She'd steered me toward a job that was a million miles away from shucking oysters at the Boudreaux Oyster Company.

We'd been living with my grandfather for over two weeks, and Pie had somehow found a hole inside his cold heart. She was trying like the dickens to squeeze inside that hole and make him like her. It pained me to see her try so hard, but he actually let her ride with him down the bayou on his pirogue today. He acted as if he was allowing Pie to tag along just to stop her from pestering him about it. When they returned she talked as if she'd rode on a float in a parade. In a way, I guess she had.

"You should have seen it, Rose," she said. "He knows how to play all kinds of songs on his fiddle, and that's how everyone knows he's coming with the oysters. They meet him on the docks and they wave at me until we get there. And Charlie showed me how he steers the boat." We'd recently discovered that Charlie was the colored boy who guided the pirogue while Antoine played his songs.

When Momma came home that night, Pie met her at the door and told her about her adventure, then she ran off to play with Radio. Momma's eyes grew soft as she looked at my grandfather sitting at the table, waxing his fiddle strings. I thought for a moment something had broken through between them. But when he noticed her looking at him, he frowned. "Why you don't tell me you name her after your mama? Why you call her dat stupid name, Pie?" And just like glass, that fragile moment shattered into a thousand pieces.

Marlene had been right about the book I'd chosen for Julia. She brought it back the next week, claiming, "I don't t'ink dat was a very good book." Well, it took everything inside me not to defend it, but then I realized she probably hadn't even read past the first page. She was the only person in Pointe-Aux-Chenes who stopped by today. And I think she only came to return the book. When she noticed *The General Foods Cookbook*, though, she checked it out. I was determined to find her a story she'd love.

With the exception of Pointe-Aux-Chenes, the other stops started to grow. We even became friends with some of the people. Mrs. Bergeron asked us into her home for lunch. We ate a bowl of hot shrimp gumbo and crusty bread. Then we admired the photos of her children that now live in Monroe.

It was exciting to discover people happy to see us pull in. Many of them were waiting when we arrived. Two families even rode in pirogues across the bayou to meet us. We stood near the water, ready to help them out of their boats. The little Arceneaux girl waved at me the entire way. While they paddled toward us, I couldn't help wondering if we had the most well-traveled books in Louisiana. If I'd really been seventeen and finished with school, I think I would have loved my job.

The next week I felt giddy with anticipation. That morning when we loaded up the bookmobile I chose a few books from the children's side and placed them on the adult side—two Nancy Drew books and one by Bess Streeter Aldrich that all the high school girls were fussing over called *Spring Came on Forever*. I was prepared to explain to Marlene why I moved them, but she didn't notice.

In Montegut, a group of people were waiting when we arrived, though I didn't see Luther or Gordie. I tried to ignore the hollow feeling inside me when we pulled away.

Julia wasn't at our stop in Pointe-Aux-Chenes. That powerful eagerness I'd felt all day sank like the *Titanic*. But a couple of minutes before it was time to pull out, Julia showed up with the cookbook in hand. "I hope dat was okay if I copied dos recipes."

"Of course," Marlene said. "How about another cookbook?"

"You got some more?"

Marlene showed her two and she settled on the one about desserts.

"Julia, can I help you find another book?" I asked. She stared at me.

I pulled out *Spring Came on Forever*. Marlene looked confused, her gaze retracing the adult section.

Julia shook her head. "No, I get dis book." She hugged the cookbook close to her chest.

"You can check out more than one book," I told her.

"Yes, Julia," said Marlene. "You sure may. And this is a good book."

Julia frowned and accepted the book as if she'd been forced into it. She seemed most happy with the cookbook.

A few minutes later, we headed back to the library. Marlene smiled at me. "I know what you did back there, Rose. You should think about going to college and becoming a librarian."

How could I tell her that thinking about it was all I was able to do?

A week later we had left Little Caillou and were on our way to Montegut when Marlene hollered, "Stop!"

What I thought was a huge log was about three yards ahead of us, blocking our way. When I looked closer I saw the short legs on the greenish black body. It was an alligator. I'd heard they were in the swamps around here, but I'd never seen one. His body stretched across the narrow road, leaving no room for us to get around him. His eyes were shut and I could see a few of his teeth even though his mouth was closed.

"Is he dead?" I asked.

"No, he's sunning." Marlene sighed. "Honk your horn." She acted like she was an expert on moving alligators across the road.

I honked and honked, but it was no use. He didn't even open his eyes. "Maybe we should back up and turn around."

Marlene settled back in her seat. "Let's stay a little bit longer. We have people waiting on us and this is the only road into town." A moment later she asked, "You don't have alligators in your part of Texas, do you?"

"No."

"What kind of varmints are out there?"

"Coyotes. They've been known to carry an entire litter of puppies away. That's how Possum found Radio."

"Radio?"

"Our dog. Possum was in the woods and this helpless little puppy had been left out there. Possum said the coyote had probably gotten the rest of the litter and was sure he'd have come back for the last one if Possum hadn't rescued him."

"Possum, Pie, Radio. Your family sure has some interesting names."

Time drags when you're waiting for an alligator to wake up and move. I thought of a song I taught Pie to sing when she jumped rope. And out there in the middle of nowhere, I started to sing, "Mumps, said the doctor. Measles, said the nurse. Vote, said the lady with the alligator purse!"

Marlene stared at me all bug-eyed. I guess I couldn't blame her. She'd never seen me act silly. By the second time around, though, she was singing with me. We sang louder and louder and darn if that old alligator didn't finally open his eyes. When he did, we screamed and clung to each other, then burst out laughing. The alligator started slowly moving across the road, dragging his long tail behind him. After he had cleared enough road that I could get around him, I held my breath and took off with a *chug-chug* and pressed down on the accelerator. My heart beat so hard I heard it pounding in my ears. When we had gone a safe distance, we exhaled together and laughed again.

"Rose, I probably shouldn't tell you this, but when I first met you, you reminded me of someone who had just gotten a good long whiff of cow manure blowing her way."

"I did?"

"Mmm-hmm. Your nose was so high in the air, if it had rained, I thought you'd surely drown." She winked, as if to soften her words.

We arrived in Montegut thirty minutes late. Only two people remained—Luther and Gordie. Luther wore a white shirt rolled up to his elbows and the sun was so bright shining down on him that I noticed the pale hairs on his tanned arms. I tried to erase my big ole grin. Luther was smiling back, though. He had a way of staring at me that made me feel naked. And I knew I shouldn't be feeling this way. He was a married man with a child.

"Hi, Gordie," I said with a little wave. "Guess what we saw today?"

Then Gordie did the most peculiar thing. He held his arms out to me and said, "Momma."

I reached for him, but Luther held him back, frowning. "That's not your momma." He blushed so it looked like a rash covering his face. "I'm sorry. His momma hasn't been able to hold him in a long time."

Gordie began to cry and kick his legs. I stood there helpless, wanting to hold him, knowing I couldn't. Marlene gave him a grape lollipop. I went to the children's side and found him a book.

Luther practically grabbed it from me and quickly picked out another Western. Then they left.

Five minutes later, we drove off. "It's the most pitiful thing," Marlene said. We rode the rest of the way to Pointe-Aux-Chenes in silence. In some ways, I was grateful for what had just happened, because it knocked me back into reality. I didn't like feeling that way about Luther, that longing for something you can't have, as if I were jumping off a cliff, hoping to land on a cloud.

When we approached our spot across from the general store, I couldn't believe my eyes. Six women stood with Julia, and they all seemed to be waiting for us.

We parked, and when we got out, Julia told me, "Dat was a good book. You got any others like dat?"

"The cookbook?" I asked.

"No," she said. "Dat story. I cried so much, my man wanted to know what happened."

"Yes," said a woman with a low, freckled forehead. "I want a book just like dat."

Marlene smiled at me, then she turned toward the woman. "Well, you can check that one out, if you'd like."

"I want one, too," said another woman. And I could tell right off that was why they were all there.

I was worried because this morning I'd placed only three books from the children's side on the adult side of the bookmobile. But Marlene must have added some, too, because she was showing the women several I hadn't even seen.

Julia and the women each chose a novel and a cookbook. And when they walked away, Marlene and I stayed there watching until we couldn't see them anymore.

Marlene smiled as she pulled down the side doors to cover the books and crawled in beside me. She didn't say a word all the way back.

As we rode toward the library my head was filled with the bayou people I'd met in the last month—Antoine, Luther, Gordie, Julia, and all the others. For a while, a pelican flew above us, his shadow becoming our temporary companion on the road. He seemed to be calling, *Follow me, follow me.*

I could hardly wait until next week.

Merle Henry

Trapped

(1957)

BLUE HAD BEEN the last puppy chosen. *The last, but the best*, thought Merle Henry. He'd gotten Blue for his twelfth birthday. A year later, the half hound, half mutt grew to a nice size and became Merle Henry's shadow, taking to the woods alongside him every morning before school to check the traps. Merle Henry wanted a mink something fierce, but all he'd trapped over the last year since he'd started were possums and raccoons.

"There goes Yip and Yap," his daddy was fond of saying when he saw Merle Henry and Blue take off for the woods.

Most nights the family read because they didn't own a television like many of their neighbors were starting to get. His daddy sat in his chair after work, reading westerns by Louis L'Amour or Zane Grey. When his mother wasn't writing in one of her Indian Chief pads, she usually read books that didn't look that interesting to Merle Henry. His seventeen-year-old brother, Gordie, read anything and everything. Merle Henry preferred *Superman* comic books, but if he read a book, it had to be exciting.

Tuesday evening the bookmobile pulled into the Hilltop Baptist Church parking lot, and Merle Henry's family drove over to select their books like they did every week. Merle Henry and Gordie sat in the back of the pickup. Blue rode with them, his head hanging over the side, his ears flapping in the wind. The cool October air felt good against Merle Henry's skin. He loved this time of year when he could be outside and not worry about mosquitoes.

When the truck stopped, the family got out. Blue wagged his tail.

"Sorry, boy," said Merle Henry. "Dogs aren't allowed in the bookmobile."

Miss Erma, the bookmobile librarian, stood to greet them, her plump hands smoothing the back of her skirt. She was chubby, but had pretty skin that always looked moist. "Hi, Luther. How ya'll doing, Rose?" she said.

"Doing just fine," Rose said. "How about you, Erma?"

Luther barely nodded. Merle Henry had once overheard his mother teasing his dad about Miss Erma. "I think she's still sweet on you," she'd said.

Merle Henry wondered if that's why his daddy didn't say much to Miss Erma. Luther was quiet around most folks, except when he'd been drinking at the Wig Wam. Then, he would let off steam like a teakettle that he'd kept simmering inside while he was sober. After he got into a fight one night, he'd promised Rose he'd stay away from the whiskey and the Wig Wam.

Tonight Merle Henry planned to choose his books quickly so he could get back to Blue.

"Here's one you might like," Miss Erma said, handing Merle Henry a book with a dog on the cover. *Old Yeller*. "Everyone's talking about it."

Merle Henry decided he'd give it a try. His brother always chose three or four, but all Gordie did was read. He didn't have a busy life like Merle Henry. Merle Henry was first and foremost a trapper. Books were merely nighttime entertainment when nothing was good on the radio.

The next morning, Merle Henry rose in the dark and dressed. He smelled the coffee dripping in the pot on the stove and heard his parents' low voices as they sat at the kitchen table. He dressed quickly and walked out of the bedroom he shared with Gordie.

"Morning, Merle Henry," Rose said, looking up from her writing pad.

"Morning, Momma." He tried not to stare at her round belly. She was expecting a baby in a few months and the sight of her expanding waistline embarrassed him for some reason, maybe because he'd overheard Luther talking with Gordie, a couple of years ago, about girls and how babies came about. Gordie hadn't seemed the least bit interested. Merle Henry tried to capture every word, listening from outside their bedroom window.

Rose stuck the pencil behind her ear. "Scrambled or fried?"

"Don't have time. I've gotta run my trap line." Merle Henry grabbed a slice of bread and his flashlight, then headed out of the kitchen and through the front door. Blue was lying on the screened porch floor, but quickly got up, ready for a walk in the woods.

Luther stood at the door, buttoning his starched work shirt. "Son, wait a second."

"Sir?"

"When I was out squirrel hunting yesterday morning, I saw where you'd placed some of those traps on foot logs. Someone could get hurt if they were crossing over."

Merle Henry was hoping that a mink might do just that, but he knew his daddy meant a person. Windstorms had caused those logs to fall, forming natural bridges across the creek. Men and boys who hunted used them. So did his cousin Faye when she was taking a shortcut from her house to theirs. The thought of having to move those traps made him want to groan. Merle Henry had worked hard attaching them to the center of the logs and covering them with moss.

"Better move them," Luther said.

"Yes, sir."

Merle Henry took off with Blue at his heels. It was dark outside. The moon looked like a lost balloon drifting between the clouds. His heart beat fast. Thoughts of mink pelts stirred in his head and his daddy's words soon left him. Maybe today would be the day he'd finally trap a mink and get twenty dollars for it from Mr. Guidry. Mr. Guidry paid only twenty-five cents for a possum pelt and fifty cents for a raccoon's. His parents let him keep all the money he made for trapping even though he was sure they could use it to help make ends meet.

Merle Henry's uncle Possum had been a great fur trapper. He gave him the traps to get started, allowing Merle Henry to pay for them as he made money from the pelts he sold. The payments stopped last fall when his mother met him after school to tell him that Uncle Possum had died from a heart attack. He'd been Merle Henry's favorite uncle and she'd known that. Rose picked him up from school that day and took him for an ice cream cone at the Whip Dip in Lecompte, the next town over. She said some days were meant for ice cream and that there was nothing Uncle Possum would have loved more than to know that his favorite nephew was eating a vanilla swirl cone in honor of him. It had taken Merle Henry a long time to wrap his mind around the fact that his uncle was dead. Possum had been only twenty-seven years old.

For the next two hours, Merle Henry and Blue checked each trap along the banks of Hurricane Creek. There was a wild smell in the woods that Merle Henry was addicted to—pine, dirt, moss. He loved to breathe it in, as if doing so made him a part of the woods, too.

This morning was a two-possum day. Merle Henry found the first one in a trap inside the base of a hollow tree and another one on a foot log near a bend in the creek. Even though they weren't minks, Merle Henry's chest felt like it would burst open. He got such a rush from it. So did Blue. His tail wagged and he barked like crazy.

Merle Henry rewarded Blue with a piece of beef jerky he kept in his pocket. Blue gobbled it up in no time.

As they headed home, the sun barely peeked between the thick pine trunks. Merle Henry hoped he'd have time to skin the possums before going to school. He passed Kappel's Nursery where the workers were already outside, watering the camellias and azaleas. As he approached the house, he noticed the truck was gone, meaning Luther had already left for his mechanic's job in Oakdale. Rose cleared the sink while Gordie ate toast and read at the table.

"How'd you do?" Rose asked.

"Two possums." Merle Henry glanced at his brother to see if he was impressed, but Gordie kept his head down and turned a page in his book.

"You want to see them, Gordie?"

His brother didn't even glance up. "I'll see them later."

Sometimes, Merle Henry thought, it was easy to tell that Gordie and he weren't full brothers. Before his parents moved to Forest Hill, his mother had married his dad in Houma when Gordie was four years old. Gordie's mother had died the year before. Maybe that was why they were so different. Gordie didn't like hunting or fishing. Come to think of it, Merle Henry had never seen him kill a fly.

"I'll take a look at your possums," Rose said, dropping the dishcloth and following Merle Henry into the front yard.

Outside, the possums hung over the fence. Blue sat underneath them like he was guarding treasure.

Rose smiled and then said, "You aren't going to try and skin them before school, are you?"

"Yes, ma'am. I have to if I'm going to keep the meat from spoiling. I want to sell them later in the colored quarters over at the sawmill town. Anyway, I have thirty minutes before the bus gets here."

Blue stood between them, panting. Merle Henry slipped his hand in his pocket and gave Blue another piece of beef jerky. He was the best trapping dog, staying with Merle Henry until the entire job was finished.

"Make sure you clean up afterwards," Rose said. "That means you and the mess. Last time, that dog of yours got into it."

Anytime Blue did something that made his mother mad she called him "that dog of yours." But he knew she liked Blue. He saw her feed him scraps from her dinner plate, and he'd seen her pet Blue's head like it was a kitten.

Merle Henry picked up his knife and Rose went inside the house.

Maybe it was the possums that made Merle Henry feel brave enough to imitate Coach Burns in P.E. He knew he shouldn't, but Merle Henry thought Coach was mean the way he called the folks who lived in the backwoods "woodsies." He said it like they were ignorant without a lick of sense. The only difference between them and the folks who lived in town was that their houses were closer to the general store and the gas station.

So when Coach Burns hadn't made it to class, Merle Henry started prancing around, his head held high like a peacock's. "Now listen here, you little woodsies, I don't care if your daddy thinks he can beat me up. I'm sure he thinks he can if he's drunk enough. But I'm from N'awlins and we are dignified there. We wait until Friday night to get good and drunk."

At first, the boys laughed hard and Merle Henry loved being in the spotlight. He kept circling the gym. Then the laughing stopped cold. A second later, Coach Burns lunged toward Merle Henry and seized hold of his earlobe and led him halfway around the basketball court.

The other boys averted their eyes. Merle Henry's face burned. As if the humiliation wasn't enough, Coach Burns ordered him to arrive at the gym at 5:30 the next morning.

"I'll keep you busy until school starts," Coach Burns said. "That is, if you live to see sunrise."

Merle Henry's ear throbbed and he decided missing out on running his trap line the next morning would be the least of his problems. He'd never been in any real trouble in school and the thought of having to tell his daddy hurt more than his ear.

That night Merle Henry went to bed early without telling his parents what had happened. He wondered if Gordie knew. If he did, he hadn't said anything about it to him. Chances were he did know. Their school was small and news traveled quickly from class to class.

In bed, Merle Henry read the rest of *Old Yeller*. He was thankful that the story let him escape from what had happened that day for a little while. He thought the ending was sad. A knot formed in Merle Henry's throat and he wondered if he would have read the book if he'd known the dog was going to die. He decided he would have, though he couldn't quite figure out why. Maybe it was because most of the book hadn't been sad. Or maybe it was because Old Yeller reminded Merle Henry of Blue.

When Gordie came into their bedroom, Merle Henry flipped over and quickly wiped his eyes with the sheet. He could hear Gordie undo his belt and slip out of his pants. Without looking, Merle Henry knew his brother would fold them up and place them on the chair at the foot of the bed. His own clothes were in a pile on the floor.

Gordie turned off the lamp on the nightstand and for a while the sounds of crickets filled the quiet between them. A moment later, Gordie asked, "How's that ear?"

An hour before dawn, Merle Henry decided he wouldn't have to tell his parents why he was leaving the house. Like most mornings, they'd assume he was running his trap line. "If nothing is in the traps, I'm going straight to school," he told them. "Coach Burns said he could use some help in the gym this morning."

It was almost the truth. He'd be going to the gym and he was certain Coach Burns would put him to work. Only the part about checking the traps had been a lie.

He hadn't counted on Blue following him. And when they got to where they entered the woods, Blue stopped and Merle Henry walked on. He turned and discovered Blue still sitting there, waiting.

"Go home, Blue. Go on home."

Blue tilted his head, looking confused. Merle Henry decided not to look back again. Blue would return home when he figured it out. Merle Henry took a few more steps. Then Blue barked. He knew Blue was trying to tell him to come on, let's go check the traps. And Merle Henry wanted to. Lord how he wanted to.

Thirty minutes later he was Coach Burns's prisoner, mopping the gym, touching up the paint in the girls' locker room. By the time the first bell rang, the gym floor sparkled and the girls' locker room walls were spotless. Every inch of Merle Henry's body ached.

"I'm not too funny now, am I, boy?" Coach Burns's furry eyebrows moved up and down like caterpillars doing push-ups.

"No, sir."

"Remember that the next time your backwoods ass wants to make fun of Marcus Burns, you hear?"

"Yes, sir."

"You're darn right."

Merle Henry couldn't wait for the day to end. On the bus, he slept with his cheek pressed against the window. He awoke when Gordie lightly shook his shoulder. "We're home."

Blue didn't meet the bus like usual, and it wasn't until Merle Henry reached the house that he remembered the last time he saw him that morning. His mother was stirring something on the stove that smelled like onions and roux. "Gumbo tomorrow night," she said. "It always tastes better the second day."

"Have you seen Blue?"

She wiped her hands on her apron. "Haven't seen hide nor hair of him all day. I was afraid he'd followed you to school."

Merle Henry dropped his books on the couch and grabbed his hatchet before taking off for the woods.

He needed to check his traps anyway. Maybe Blue was still out there, waiting for him. He ran to the spot on the road where Blue had been that morning, then quickly tore into the woods. He passed the first trap. It was empty. He felt dizzy and his breathing became shallow. Then he passed the second one even though there was a possum between the trap's jaws. Today it could have been a mink and he would have still left it behind, because now he was in the woods for one reason only.

As he approached the trap by the foot log he heard a whining sound. Merle Henry froze when he saw the familiar blue-gray hair. A sour taste filled his mouth, and he heard his father's warning playing over in his head. *Better move those traps off the foot logs. Better move those traps. Better move those traps.*

Blue's left hind leg was trapped and his upper body was caught between two narrow limbs branching off the thick log. He was grateful for those limbs. They kept Blue from drowning.

Blue looked weakly over at Merle Henry, but he didn't bark, he just whined. Merle Henry raced toward the log. When he reached it, he walked slowly across until he got to Blue. Then he sat, his legs straddling the log, and tried to open the jaws of the trap.

Blue snapped at him.

Merle Henry pulled his hand away, then said, "It's okay, boy. It's okay."

Holding the chain, he gently raised Blue and the trap between the branches and placed him on the log. Blue's leg was covered in blood.

Merle Henry's hand shook, but he dug for a piece of beef jerky in his pocket and offered it to Blue. Usually it disappeared, but today Blue just stared at it.

"Come on, Blue. You like it. You know you do."

Blue licked the jerky, but he wouldn't eat. Merle Henry slid off the log and stood waist deep in the icy cold water. He grabbed his hatchet. His hands shook as he tried to undo the staple that held the chain to the underside of the log. Finally the staple gave way and freed the chain.

Merle Henry unbuttoned his shirt, slipped it off, and placed it flat on the log. Then he carefully lifted Blue, who was still attached to the trap. The trap's jaw had torn Blue's hair and flesh and probably part of the bone. Merle Henry couldn't tell for sure because of the blood. He laid Blue on top of his shirt and slowly formed a sling.

Blue made a low growling sound while Merle Henry found his way out of the woods and back to the road, walking slowly so he didn't hurt Blue any more than he already had. The chain dangled, hitting Merle Henry's leg with each step. Cold air hit his bare chest and soaked pants. But he didn't care. A lump gathered in his throat. He tried not to think of *Old Yeller*. He would do everything he could to make this right and not end like that story.

Luther's truck was parked in front of the house. Gordie was in the yard, chopping wood. When Merle Henry made it to the path leading up to their house, Gordie dropped the ax and ran toward the porch.

"Momma! Daddy!" Gordie called from the steps.

By the time Merle Henry reached the truck, everyone was outside.

"Can I take him to Doc Harrison's?" Gordie asked.

"We don't have any money to pay the Doc," Luther said. "We're already going to owe for the baby."

"I'll pay him, Daddy." Merle Henry had some trapping money saved and now knew how to mop and paint.

Luther tossed Gordie the keys. "I don't think it's any use, but go ahead."

Merle Henry looked down at the shirt that was covered in Blue's blood and understood why Luther didn't think there was any hope.

Rose covered her mouth with one hand and rested the other on her belly.

Gordie started the truck and their parents walked over to Merle Henry's side.

"Here, let me hold him while you get in," Luther said, taking the sling with Blue from Merle Henry. After he gave him back, Rose reached inside and stroked Blue's head. The pencil dropped from behind her ear, and she gasped, catching it before it hit Blue.

The ride to Glenmora was only about five miles by way of Cut Off Road, but it seemed a hundred miles away today. For once, Merle Henry was thankful for his quiet brother because the last thing he wanted to do was answer questions about what had happened. As they cruised down the dirt road, the tall pine trees became a blur of brown and green. They reached Doc Harrison's as he was locking his office door.

Gordie jumped out of the truck first. "Doc, we have a hurt dog. Could you take a look?"

The doctor looked at Merle Henry, who had

stepped out of the truck, holding Blue in his bloody shirt. "Good God, boys. Did he get run over?"

"No," Merle Henry said. "He got caught in a trap. One of my traps."

Doc unlocked the door and held it open. "Come on. I'm not a veterinarian, but I'll see what I can do."

A few minutes later, Doc gave Blue a shot and the hound grew sleepy enough for Doc to release the trap's tight hold. With Blue stretched out on the examination table, Merle Henry could see the lower leg was barely attached to Blue's body. "Gordie, take your brother and go on home. I'm not going to make any promises. This doesn't look good."

Gordie touched Merle Henry's arm. "Come on."

Merle Henry stayed put, not wanting to move. Not wanting to leave his best friend.

Doc Harrison frowned. "There's nothing you can do here. I'll let you know something tomorrow."

"We'll have to call you," said Merle Henry. "We don't have a phone."

While they rode in silence back to the house, Merle Henry held on to the dashboard, wishing he was like Gordie, satisfied reading instead of trapping.

When they parked in front of the house, Merle Henry's throat closed up. Then he swallowed and asked, "Do you think Doc will have to shoot him?"

Gordie shook his head. "No. Doctors have medicine that can put animals to sleep."

"Forever?"

"Forever."

Somehow Merle Henry knew Gordie wasn't telling the whole truth, but he wanted to believe that if Blue couldn't be with him, he could have sweet dreams for eternity.

Merle Henry's legs felt heavy as he reached the porch steps. When Rose met him at the front door with her arms wide open, he fell into her embrace and cried. Over his momma's shoulder, Merle Henry saw Luther turn and walk out of the room.

"Daddy told me to move those traps, and I didn't. I should have done it."

Rose patted his back and said, "I think that gumbo might be ready after all."

Merle Henry couldn't eat, but guilt was eating him up inside. Finally he told his parents what he should have earlier. He told them what happened at school with Coach Burns and how he was caught imitating him, repeating comments he always made about the people that lived deep in the woods. Somehow it all seemed connected to what had happened to Blue. He wanted to blame Coach Burns, but he knew it was his own fault.

As he listened, Luther's temples pulsed and his jaw tensed. Merle Henry wondered if his rear end was about to meet the belt.

"Burns said what?" Luther roared.

"He called us woodsies. He said the men get drunk at the Wig Wam every night."

"Calm down, Luther," Rose said. "You know how he thinks he's something because he's from New Orleans. Only I know he's not. His people are from Chalmette, and that is not New Orleans."

Her words didn't seem to work on Luther, who looked like he could spit nails.

For a minute, Merle Henry was relieved to see his daddy get all worked up about Coach Burns. But then his thoughts returned to Blue and he knew nothing on this earth could replace the pain of losing him.

"Merle Henry, I'll fix you a bath," Rose said, "after everyone is out of the kitchen."

Luther pulled away from the table and stood. "I'm going out for a while."

A second later, the front door slammed and Merle Henry heard Rose say, "Oh, mercy."

Later that evening, lying in bed, Merle Henry was wishing they had a telephone. Finally he realized it wouldn't matter if they did. Doctors probably never made late-night calls about dogs.

Merle Henry didn't want to go to school the next day, but his mother made him. "Can't we walk to Faye's and call Doc Harrison first?"

"It's too early to call. His office isn't open yet."

Merle Henry noticed that his daddy wasn't at the kitchen table and when he saw the truck parked out front he asked, "Where's Daddy?"

Then he heard the loud snoring from his parents' bedroom.

Rose frowned. "He has one of his headaches. You better tell Gordie it's time to go out and wait for the bus."

Merle Henry started for the bedroom.

"Just a second, son."

He turned.

Rose sighed. "There comes a time in life where you have to pay for the choices you make. I think you learned that yesterday."

Merle Henry lowered his head. "Yes, ma'am."

By P.E. class Merle Henry knew that Coach Burns wouldn't be there. He'd learned that the coach had lost a fight at the Wig Wam with some man from the backwoods. Merle Henry remembered how his daddy had left the house last night. Normally the thought of his daddy beating up Coach Burns would have made him puff up with pride. Today he couldn't think of anything but Blue.

When school let out, he headed to the bus like usual. Then he heard someone call, "Merle Henry!" Rose stood in front of the truck. She was too far away from him to tell whether she appeared sad or not. All he could see was her brown hair blowing in the breeze and a flower apron covering her big bump. He moved slowly toward her, fearing the reason she was there, already knowing. It was just like the time she met him after school to tell him about Uncle Possum. Today, though, Merle Henry didn't feel much like eating a vanilla swirl cone. He didn't care if he ever trapped a mink, possum, or squirrel. He'd never go into the woods again.

He reached his mother and stared down at her worn shoes, afraid to look at her face.

Lifting his chin with her hand, she smiled softly at him. She smelled like Camay soap. "Come here."

Rose wrapped her arm around his shoulders and even though Merle Henry was thirteen he let her guide him to the passenger side of the truck. He didn't care if anyone saw them. When she opened the door he stared at a cardboard box on the seat.

"Blue!" Merle Henry reached down to touch him.

Blue licked his hand and his tail thumped against the side of the box. What was left of his injured leg had been bandaged with layers of white tape.

Merle Henry looked up at his mother. Her smile was so big, he could see her teeth.

"You'll have to work for Doc a little while, Merle Henry. Maybe you can offer to keep his place clean or mow his lawn."

"Yes, ma'am, I will."

"He said we didn't owe him anything, but Harps pay their debts. All of them. Your daddy is having to pay for his right now."

He wanted to ask what she meant by that, but Gordie was walking toward them and Merle Henry was eager to see what his brother would say when he discovered Blue.

Merle Henry slid over to the middle of the seat and carefully placed the box on his lap. Gordie opened the truck door and ducked his head inside, then froze. "Well, I'll be," he said, and for someone who didn't say much, that was saying a lot.

Rose started the engine and pulled out of the

parking lot where the last of the kids were running toward the buses. The sun was shining mighty bright that afternoon, but even if it wasn't, it would have felt that way to Merle Henry. Today anything was possible. He could fly to the stars, if he wanted. "Momma, can we get ice cream at the Whip Dip?"

Rose smiled. "Merle Henry, that's a good idea. Some days are meant for ice cream. I believe this is one of them."

Playing Hooky

(1958)

LILY BEA WAS the prettiest girl Merle Henry had ever seen. She had brown eyes that reminded him of the doe he'd shot last winter. And her hair was golden like the bales of hay in Mr. Cantry's field up the road. He bet she smelled good, too, but he'd never been close enough to her to know for sure. He still couldn't believe she was going to the Sweetheart Dance with him. He'd never dreamed she'd say yes. Tommy had asked for him because Merle Henry was scared Lily Bea might say no.

Now he was scared because she'd said yes. If he didn't do something quick, he'd be going to the Forest Hill School Sweetheart Dance with two left feet. This was the first year eighth-graders were allowed to go and he'd concentrated so hard on getting up the nerve to convince Tommy to ask Lily Bea for him that he'd forgotten he didn't know how to dance.

The dance was two days away and he still hadn't cracked open *The Tango and Other Up-to-Date Dances.* He'd checked it out of the bookmobile a couple of weeks ago. He didn't go with his family as he usually did on Tuesday nights. He waited until they returned, then he walked the two miles with Blue hobbling behind on his three legs. The almost full moon was big and low in the sky that night. Merle Henry was grateful for the light it provided since he left his flashlight at home. Except for the giant longleaf pines, it seemed like he and Blue were the only things out there.

Arriving at the Hilltop Baptist Church parking lot, he waited until no one was in the bookmobile. Later when he handed Miss Erma the book, she'd said, "Your daddy sure could dance. Whoo-ee! You ought to ask Luther how to cut a rug."

His face warmed and he said, "It's for a report I'm doing."

"We didn't have any classes like that when I was in school with Luther. Say, isn't that Sweetheart

Dance coming up soon?" She winked at him like she knew exactly why he was checking out that book.

He walked home with the book hidden under his jacket, wondering all the way back how Miss Erma knew Luther could dance so well. She was kind of pretty, but he didn't like thinking of anyone dancing with his daddy except his momma. He looked down at his hound. "You're lucky, Blue. No she-dog will ever expect you to cut a rug."

Blue did know how to twirl around in a circle, something he'd never done until he'd lost that hind leg.

Merle Henry's aunt Pie would be visiting this afternoon from Alexandria. She was only five years younger than his momma, but she seemed a lot younger.

"I'm a grass widow," she was fond of saying when people asked her about her husband.

"That's another way of saying divorced," his daddy explained to Merle Henry the first time he'd heard Aunt Pie say it. "They're separated by miles and miles of grass. Pie is like a stray cat, always looking for a better fish."

Merle Henry thought Aunt Pie was pure-d fun.

She'd taken him to the Louisiana State Fair last year in Shreveport. They rode every ride three times and gawked at all the sideshows. She even entered the watermelon-seed spitting contest and won. Aunt Pie had a round face and a little rump that twisted side to side when she walked. And when she laughed, her whole face laughed, including her eyes, which grew tiny and reminded Merle Henry of a cute little possum's. He hoped he could have a girlfriend like Aunt Pie one of these days. For now, he'd make do with Lily Bea. That is, if he didn't lose his shot with her by not knowing how to dance.

In the afternoon, Merle Henry waited for Aunt Pie's arrival, while chopping wood out front. He wore a T-shirt, hoping to impress her with the new muscles he'd noticed in the mirror recently. Now the damp shirt stuck to his skin from sweat. He was thinking about changing when Aunt Pie rode up with a red-headed fellow in an army jeep. Merle Henry wanted to escape inside the house. He hadn't liked her last boyfriend, Buck, a car salesman from Lake Charles who told stupid jokes, then socked Merle Henry's shoulder as if to emphasize the punch line. "Get it?" Buck would say.

Merle Henry's arm hurt an entire week following

their visit. When they'd driven off, his mother had said, "Mercy, Pie can surely do better than that."

And when Aunt Pie showed up alone the next weekend with a black eye, *she* decided she could do better.

"What did he do to you?" his mother had asked, handing Pie a dishcloth filled with ice chips.

"You should see *him*, Rose," said Aunt Pie. "Mr. Fancy Pants won't be flashing that snazzy grin until he gets that tooth replaced." Then she laughed and soon Rose joined her.

That day Merle Henry had wanted to kill Buck.

Today when the soldier boy parked, Aunt Pie jumped out of the jeep, and Merle Henry kept chopping wood. Pie's hair looked blonder than usual and she wore red high heels and a circle skirt like some of the girls from school.

"Merle Henry, is that you? Come give your aunt Pie a hug." She held out her arms wide as if she was trying to grab all the air around them.

Merle Henry gave her a quick hug. The skinny red-headed soldier was standing right behind Aunt Pie, grinning. With a closer look, Merle Henry thought the soldier looked the same age as Gordie, who was a senior this year.

Aunt Pie swung around and slipped her arm through the soldier's. "This is Cooter."

Cooter held out his hand to Merle Henry. Merle Henry shook it hard, trying to show all his strength.

When Merle Henry released his hand, Cooter rubbed his fingers. "Goodness, that's some shake you have there, buddy. Remind me not to get on your bad side."

Aunt Pie laughed and Merle Henry's face felt flushed. "Where's your momma?" she asked.

But before Merle Henry could holler for her, she was standing in the doorway, an apron tied above her huge melon belly.

"Hey there, Pie." She reached over and kissed Aunt Pie's cheek.

Aunt Pie looked down at Rose's stomach. "Mercy, Rose. You're as big as a house." She patted Momma's apron.

"It won't be too long," said Rose. "Doc says a month, but I don't know about his arithmetic."

"You look beautiful," Aunt Pie said. "Maybe this time it will be a girl." Then she seemed to notice Rose staring at her friend.

"This is Cooter," she added, slipping her arm through his again.

Cooter took off his uniform hat. "Pleased to meet you, ma'am."

Rose looked startled. Merle Henry wondered if it was because she'd fried only one chicken and fretted that there wouldn't be enough for everyone or if she was noticing how young Cooter looked.

"Come on in." Rose led the way into the house. "We'll go ahead and eat. Luther is working a little late."

They listened to Aunt Pie talk at the dinner table about how she'd met Cooter when she got hired to run errands at Fort Polk. "Then this cute red-headed thing asked me to a dance at the enlisted men's club. And you know how I like to dance, Rose."

Merle Henry suddenly felt a stab in his gut.

That night Luther came home with some beer and offered Cooter one, but not before asking, "You are old enough, aren't you, son?"

Cooter grinned. "Yes, sir. I just have a baby face."

"How old are you?" Merle Henry asked, knowing good and well he shouldn't have. He expected his momma or daddy to snap at him, or at least give one of their disapproving looks, but they just stared at Cooter, waiting for an answer.

Before he could say a word, Aunt Pie grabbed Cooter's hand and pulled him to the floor. "Old enough to dance," she said. "Gordie, turn that radio up."

Gordie had been reading the newspaper. He leaned over and turned up the volume, and everyone watched Aunt Pie and Cooter move around the little living room floor to the music coming from KALB radio. Merle Henry tried to memorize every step they took.

The next morning Merle Henry woke to a plan. Maybe it was because he'd dreamed about dancing with Lily Bea around the gym floor. He decided he'd play hooky and stay home to study that dance book. After watching Aunt Pie and Cooter dance for a few songs, it was bound to click with him. And if it didn't, he'd just be sick the next day, too. That idea sounded like the best yet. He'd get out of dancing, and keep Lily Bea from going with anyone else since it was too late for her to get another date. Maybe she'd even feel sorry for him and bake him a lemon cake or peanut butter cookies. Or she might get real mad and not ever talk to him again.

He hadn't really talked to her much anyway. Tommy had done the talking and he didn't seem to mind at all. Merle Henry had watched him speaking to Lily Bea from across the cafeteria and they got along just fine. Remembering that now caused Merle Henry to open the book and start studying.

The only thing nagging Merle Henry about playing hooky was that he couldn't run his trap line. And though he'd trapped eighteen possums, and three raccoons, he still hadn't caught a mink.

Twenty minutes later, Gordie was already dressed and out of their room. The morning was nippy like most February mornings in Forest Hill, that wet morning chill that comes from so much humidity. Merle Henry hid the book under his pillow and raised the sheet until it reached his chin.

Rose cracked open the door. "Merle Henry, you're running late. You're gonna have to walk to school if you don't hurry up."

Merle Henry let out a groan. "Momma, I don't feel so good." He hadn't played hooky since second grade and his mother had known all along that he was pretending. Back then, she had let him stay home, but she'd given him so many chores, he decided playing hooky wasn't that much fun.

Rose walked over to him and touched his forehead. She raised an eyebrow. "You don't have a fever."

"It's my belly. I feel kind of sick."

She let out a sigh. "You're not the only one. Cooter must have hugged the toilet in the outhouse on and off all night. Nobody can out-drink your daddy."

"Cooter and Aunt Pie are still here?"

"Mm-hm. It was like musical beds last night. Pie and I slept in my room, and your daddy slept on the couch. Cooter just conked out wherever he landed."

Rose picked up Merle Henry's pants off the floor and folded them. "I guess you want to stay home. You do remember that dance is tomorrow night?"

"Yes, ma'am."

She placed his pants on the end of his bed. "I suspect you better stay home or you might break that little Lily Bea's heart if you're sick tomorrow. Although I think you're too young to get sweet on a girl."

His mother was always talking about how she wanted her boys to go to college. "You could be something great," she'd say. "Maybe even a writer." Merle Henry wanted to tell her that going to college and becoming a writer were not in his future plans.

After Rose eased the door closed, he heard his brother leave the house for school. Soon Merle Henry could concentrate on learning to dance, but his mind was on those traps.

A few minutes later, Rose appeared again. "Blue

is whining something awful. You think he's missing the woods?"

"Yes, ma'am. I sure do."

"Well, I've got to go over to Faye's this morning. She got into a mess of poison ivy. I'll go the short way through the woods and check on your traps. If you have anything, I'm sure Gordie or your daddy will take care of it later today."

Maybe Daddy, thought Merle Henry. Never Gordie. It amazed him how his mother still didn't realize how different Gordie was from him.

Before she left for Faye's, she said, "If you need anything, Pie will help you. I guess you better tell me where to find your traps."

An hour later, Merle Henry heard Aunt Pie and Cooter in the kitchen.

"I'll make you some eggs, Cooter," she said.

Cooter groaned. "That's the last thing I want."

"I know what you need."

"What's that?"

"A good shot of whiskey," said Aunt Pie.

"Oooh, no, ma'am. Thank you. That's what got me into this mess."

"Well, I warned you. You should have stuck to the dancing."

Her words brought Merle Henry back to why he was home. He opened the book, then started to read and study the pictures. There was no way he was going to learn to dance just by reading. He threw the sheets back and stood on the floor, holding the book straight in front of his eyes. If the book was going to be his dancing partner, he'd have to give her a name.

"How you doing, Matilda?" he said to the open page. "Some nice words you got there."

Suddenly he heard someone snicker. He swung around and discovered Aunt Pie in the doorway. Her hand covered her mouth, but Merle Henry could tell she was smiling by the way her eyes had shrunk into tiny slits.

He dropped the book. His ears burned like the day Coach had hold of one of them. His stomach was starting to really ache now.

"Oh, Merle Henry, I wasn't making fun of you. I just never heard of a dancing partner named Matilda. Maybe Carol Ann or Suzie or Joyce Lynn."

Merle Henry turned his head and gazed out the window. He didn't want Aunt Pie to think he was a fool that talked and danced with books.

Aunt Pie walked over to him and picked up the book. She read the title and flipped the book open to the front page. She started to laugh again. "I'm sorry, but, Merle Henry, this book was written in 1914. That's over forty years ago. Why didn't you tell me you wanted to learn to dance? I can teach you."

Merle Henry didn't say anything. He just stared at the floor.

She had one hand resting on her hip and the other stretched toward him. "Well, are you going to ignore a lady offering to teach you to dance?"

"But I'm supposed to be sick."

"Yes, sir, I can see that." She was smiling at him and now Merle Henry smiled back.

"But Momma will—"

"Oh, she'll be gone for a while. Besides, we've got the same genes. You're bound to be a fast learner."

Grabbing his hand, she led him out to the living room where Cooter was laying on the couch, a washcloth over his head. She flipped on the radio. A tune played that he didn't recognize, but the song had a good beat.

"Does that have to be so loud?" Cooter asked, his hands protecting his ears. He sounded like a whiney little boy to Merle Henry. Aunt Pie sure could pick them!

Aunt Pie sighed. "Cooter, do yourself a favor and take a good long swig of that Jack Daniel's. I'm telling you, I know what I'm talking about."

Cooter pulled the washcloth from his forehead and opened his eyes. "You mean you've been in this state before?"

"Never. But I've known plenty of men who have."

Pie placed one of Merle Henry's hands on her waist and the other on her shoulder. "Now, Merle Henry, pretend I'm your girl. Follow me, and soon I'll be following you."

"Are you sure I should do that?"

She threw her head back and laughed. "I'm sure, honey. You're the man. You're supposed to lead."

For the first three songs, Merle Henry was her shadow, following her steps and listening to the music and her voice carry him through the song. "One, two, three," she said, first loudly, then by the third song the words came out in a whisper. Aunt Pie's voice was spun sugar on a paper cone. Merle Henry heard it as if it were his own heart beating. And standing this near, he could smell her sweet perfume.

At first his hands felt like putty and his feet were heavy as bricks, but by the fifth song he was leading, spinning her around the room.

"Oh no," Cooter cried, rushing off for the out-house.

When he returned, they were slowing their pace

to a ballad. Cooter braced the doorway. "Where's that whiskey?"

"In the Ritz Cracker canister over the sink," said Aunt Pie. She kept her gaze on Merle Henry and never missed a step.

Merle Henry thought it was nice that Aunt Pie knew where to find things in their house. It kind of made it her home, too. She never stayed in one place long anyway.

An hour and a half later, Aunt Pie stopped moving and dropped her arms to her sides. "Young man, you've worn me out. You're going to be the most dashing gentleman at that school dance."

Merle Henry beamed as if he were six feet tall.

She raised an eyebrow. "You aren't sick at all, are you?"

"No, ma'am."

"Cooter's more sick than you."

"I'm starting to feel better," Cooter said, now sitting up on the couch. "That whiskey does do the trick. And I'm not drunk either."

Aunt Pie flopped on the couch beside him. "I doubt you will be for a while." She combed her fingers through his hair. "If you know what's good for you, sugar, you'll remember this morning."

Merle Henry's feet tingled. They wanted to keep moving. Aunt Pie was right, dancing was in his genes. He'd never seen his parents dance even though they said they used to dance in Houma every Friday night. He felt like they'd been keeping an important secret from him. Gordie never danced, but he didn't seem interested. Girls were always making goo-goo eyes at Gordie, and Merle Henry had seen him sneaking looks at girls. But Gordie was probably too shy to ask someone to the dance. Then again, Merle Henry hadn't exactly asked anyone either.

Aunt Pie picked up the Indian Chief notepad on the end table and thumbed through the pages like someone shuffling a deck of cards. "Does your momma still write those stories?"

Merle Henry pointed to a box in the corner, filled with dozens of notepads. "What do you think?"

"I wonder where your momma is," Aunt Pie asked, looking at the clock.

"She went to Faye's house. Remember?" Merle Henry said.

"But that was two hours ago. Rose told me she was just taking a bottle of chamomile lotion to Faye."

"You could call her," offered Merle Henry. Merle Henry's family had finally gotten a telephone the month before when his father started worrying about the baby coming and him working all the way in Oakdale. And it hadn't cost too much since they shared a party line with eight other families.

"Good idea." Aunt Pie dialed Faye's number. She talked a few minutes about meeting Cooter and her new job at Fort Polk and how she was getting a chance to go hear Johnny Cash sing. Then she asked if Rose was still there. As she listened, her eyes grew wide.

"I better go," Aunt Pie said and quickly hung up.

"What's wrong?" Merle Henry asked.

"Rose never made it over there."

Merle Henry tried to swallow the big lump gathering in his throat. Finally, he said, "She might be in the woods. She was going to check my traps on the way to Faye's house."

Aunt Pie bit her lower lip and yanked on her hair. "Lord, I hope she didn't fall. Maybe she's having the baby out there. Oh, mercy, what do we do?"

Merle Henry wished Aunt Pie would shut up. All her chatter was making him nervous. How could the magic he felt just a moment ago be swept away with one big swoosh?

"Now hold on," Cooter said, standing. "Let's think calmly."

In that instant, Merle Henry changed his mind about Cooter. He was glad he was there. Someone needed to think calmly. Talking crazy like Aunt Pie wasn't going to help his mother.

"I know the way to the woods," Merle Henry said. "I'll just be a second."

He ran to his room and changed into his pants and shirt. If anything happened to his mother he'd never forgive himself. He was the reason she went through the woods. Sometimes she chose to go that way to Faye's, but maybe she wouldn't have today. Thoughts spun in his head. He rushed past Aunt Pie and Cooter, and headed toward the front door.

"Wait for us," hollered Aunt Pie, racing after him.

"You better stay put," Cooter told her. "Rose might come back and if she sees all of us gone, she'll worry."

Aunt Pie stepped off the front porch anyway.

They didn't need to go much farther, though. Rose was walking toward them. She had a quick pace, and Blue was trying to keep up with her, his tail aimed toward the sky. As she came closer, Merle Henry noticed something small and dark in her hand.

"It's a mink!" Rose hollered. "I got the mink!" She held the fur up high in the air.

Merle Henry thought he was about to lose his wits. Since last year he'd tried to get a mink, wanted it more than anything, and now his momma was practically skipping toward him with a mink in her hand. He knew he should be relieved to see her alive and safe, but he felt something rising inside him that wanted to explode.

"Well, hot damn!" yelled Cooter. "Your momma is something else. She can fry chicken and trap a mink!"

Rose was so close now Merle Henry could see the mink's beady eyes. "Oh, I didn't trap this mink. That young man standing next to you trapped it. I just happened on him. He was half drowned when I found him."

Aunt Pie's eyes grew big. "You mean he was still alive?"

Merle Henry was starting to think Pie's hair was too blond and her eyes too small. She was more appealing when she was quiet and dancing.

"He sure was alive," Rose said. "I thought to myself, now what would Merle Henry do? And I realized, well, he'd put that poor mink out of its misery."

"You shot him?" Cooter asked. He was clinging to her every word.

"No! I don't have a gun. I found a forked stick and held his head under the water until he finished drowning. I thought he'd never die."

Merle Henry felt numb.

Rose looked up at him. "Did I do right, son?"

Merle Henry looked at his momma standing there with that mink in her hand. Her hair was wild, and her dress had smudges of dirt. His brother would never have done it, but his momma did. She did it for him because she knew how much he'd wanted a mink. And she was right. He did trap it, after all. She was just delivering it to him.

"You did just fine, Momma. Now hand that mink over to me so I can dress it out."

"Aren't you sick?" she asked, so bewildered that Merle Henry realized she had believed him.

"I've had a miraculous recovery," Merle Henry said, taking the mink from her. It really was a beautiful sight.

Blue barked and twirled in a circle, as if he were part of something special.

Aunt Pie laughed. "Well, look at Blue. Even he has our family's dancing genes!"

Annabeth

Fairy Tale

(1973)

ANNABETH WAS READY to kill her brother.

"How to Be Popular, by Annabeth Harp." Ryan's voice came from the back porch.

"One: Smile all the time unless your friends say something sad." Ryan announced each word loud enough for their grandmother's neighbors to hear two acres away.

By the time Annabeth arrived at the back porch, Ryan had escaped somewhere else. She should have known better than to leave the list under her pillow. And to think she'd been concerned about Gamma Rose's discovering it. She hated the thought of her practical grandmother thinking she was silly and concerned about frivolous things like being popular.

But after what happened at school last year, she was going to make sure eighth grade at her new school was different.

"Two: Join clubs and run for an office," Ryan hollered from the front porch now. Annabeth dashed past her grandmother in the kitchen and headed toward the porch where she discovered Ryan had already fled.

What happened last September had ruined the entire year. If she'd only known she might start her period that day, she'd never have worn white jeans. Before that she'd felt invisible. By the end of the day, everyone knew her name. One moment was so fragile, so important.

Next year, she'd be prepared. When she left Gamma Rose's she'd have memorized her how-to-be-popular list. And she'd be tanned. Having a tan might make that possible. At least her thighs would look thinner.

"Three: If a boy tries to kiss you, let him, unless he has mono. Four—" Ryan yelled, but he didn't finish because Gamma Rose grabbed him by the arm and snatched the paper. With an outstretched arm, she continued holding squatty Ryan by the wrist. Gamma Rose's black pants and blouse made her look even slimmer and taller than she was already. And the contrast between her and Ryan made Annabeth think of a pilgrim showing off a plump turkey for a Thanksgiving meal.

Without looking at the list, Gamma Rose returned it to Annabeth, who was trying to resist punching her brother.

Gamma Rose released Ryan. "It's Tuesday," she said. "Let's go to the bookmobile."

Relieved to have something else to think about, Annabeth walked by her brother and pinched him in his chubby gut.

"Ouch! Hey, Gamma Rose, did you see that?"

Gamma Rose's eyebrows shot up. "Yes, I did. And frankly I would have belted you one if I was your sister." She unsnapped her purse and slid the pink frosty lipstick over her lips.

Annabeth gathered her books from last week and joined her brother and grandmother in the old Buick warming up outside. She loved going to the bookmobile, even though the selection was small compared to her junior high library in Gretna. It made her think about how her mother and dad had gone to the same spot each Tuesday. Even Miss Erma was the same librarian at the bookmobile back then. Annabeth's dad had told her Miss Erma had been kind of pretty years ago, but now Miss Erma was plump and wore glasses as thick as Coke bottles. A pencil always stuck out of her loose bun.

On the ride over, Ryan stared out the window, staying quiet in the backseat. Annabeth wondered if Gamma Rose's comment had embarrassed him or if he was planning another scheme to torture her. She'd tried to be a little more patient with Ryan since things had been so bad at home. Her dad had lost his job again, and this time they had to sell their home. Her parents sent them to Gamma Rose's while they moved to a rent house in Marrero, another suburb on the New Orleans Westbank. Her mom had been upset about losing their home, but for Annabeth the move meant a new school and maybe a new life.

Gamma Rose drove fast. When they came to the hilly parts, it felt as if the wheels were flying above the road. "I wonder if Merle Henry will call tonight?"

Annabeth thought it sounded strange to hear her dad referred to as Merle Henry. He'd dropped the Henry part a long time ago, just like her mother now went by Lily instead of Lily Bea.

They pulled into the Hilltop Baptist Church parking lot where the bookmobile parked. The Buick's tires crunched the gravel as they found a place to stop. Ryan jumped out and ran ahead.

"I'll take your books for you, Gamma Rose," Annabeth offered.

Gamma Rose shook her head. "I can carry them. That's why I brought this tote. Haven't lost all my strength." Then she added, "Yet."

"Hello, Rose," Miss Erma said.

"Morning, Erma. Doesn't look as if the weather-man is going to get his rain."

"Nope," said Miss Erma. "I've learned to just check my cat instead of listening to the weather reports."

"How do you check your cat?" Ryan asked.

"If she's licking her face, it's a sure sign we're going to get some rain." Miss Erma held up a book. "I've got a new animal story for you, Ryan. I remember someone else who liked to read animal books. I sure miss him."

"I do, too," said Gamma Rose. Luther had died the year before in a car accident, driving back from Alexandria.

Miss Erma handed the book to Ryan. "Your daddy, Merle Henry, used to like animal stories, too."

"I know," Ryan said. "He gave me *Old Yeller* for my birthday."

"That's a good one," Miss Erma said.

Annabeth felt sorry for Miss Erma. She wondered

when Miss Erma had turned into a plump book-mobile librarian.

Annabeth sucked in her stomach. That wouldn't happen to her. By the time her parents returned, she would have changed herself into a new person. She'd go by her middle name, if she had one. She could be just Beth. She didn't feel like a Beth, though. *Beth* made her think of the meek character in *Little Women*. At least she didn't want to feel like a Beth.

She thumbed through the two fairy-tale books in the bookmobile. She knew she was getting too old to read about Cinderella and Snow White, but she still yearned for magical moments. And as if she'd read her mind, her grandmother said, "I've always loved a good fairy tale myself."

Annabeth smiled.

"The only thing is," said Gamma Rose, "firstborn girls sure get treated shabby in those stories."

That was true, Annabeth thought. It always seemed like the older sisters were ugly and cruel.

"Well, maybe with a few exceptions," added Gamma Rose. "Rapunzel and Sleeping Beauty were firstborns, weren't they?"

"Yes," Annabeth said. "Well, I think they were only children." Annabeth glanced over to Ryan, who was pulling yet another book off the shelf, making a mess on the floor. He acted as if he were two years old instead of nine. Being an only child was a heavenly thought right now.

Annabeth chose a thick volume of Hans Christian Andersen's fairy tales. In fourth grade she'd read a biography on Andersen and learned how he was an ugly duckling. She'd felt that way herself last year.

Back at Gamma Rose's house, her grandmother asked Annabeth to turn on the oven timer for thirty minutes, then she said, "No, make that twenty-five."

I wish life was like that, thought Annabeth. If she could turn back time and make things different, she'd have never chosen to wear white jeans that day. They had been brand-new. Before she left for school, she'd checked herself in the mirror and decided she looked cool. If only she'd known what would happen in a few hours.

Annabeth changed into her bathing suit and spread a mixture of iodine and baby oil over her body. With the fairy-tale book in hand, she stretched out on her stomach atop a towel in the front yard. Once comfortable, she glanced at her watch. Four o'clock. She'd have to remember to flip over at 4:30.

A few pages into "Thumbelina," she heard a galloping sound on the road that ran in front of her grandmother's house. Soon a young man on a white horse appeared. She liked the way the boy rode, confident and free. A few minutes later, he passed again. Even though the house was a good distance from the road, she thought she noticed him turn his head and look her way.

"Who is that boy?" she asked Gamma Rose, now sitting on the porch swing, sipping a glass of iced tea.

"That's Tommy Hopkins's boy. He and his wife adopted him when he was just a baby. He's a show-off, but he can sure ride a horse."

"How old is he?"

"Goodness, child. I don't know. Seems just the other day he was a little thing going to vacation Bible school." After a quick pause, she added, "I expect he's about high school age. Funny, I can't remember that boy's first name." She snapped her tongue and shook her head.

The next day, Annabeth was tanning in the front yard, reading, when the boy passed by again at four sharp. This time, his horse walked with a high-stepping gait. Gamma Rose was right. He was a show-off. But the following day, Annabeth found herself making her way to the front yard around four in the afternoon.

When Gamma Rose saw her dressed in her bathing suit, she said, "You sure you're not getting too much sun? You're looking kind of red to me."

"I'm fine," Annabeth said. "I have to burn a little before it turns into a tan."

Gamma Rose shook her head. "In my day, we didn't want to have a tan."

Annabeth ignored her remark and went outside. When the boy passed this time, she made her way to the mailbox on the other side of the road, timing it perfectly so that when the boy reached the mailbox, she'd be there. Now she felt stupid standing, mail in hand, waiting. She also felt naked when she realized she was wearing her bathing suit, even though it was a one-piece. For a second, she thought of dashing back to the house to slip on a pair of shorts, but quickly changed her mind because she'd risk missing him ride back by. After thumbing through the mail a few minutes, she started moving at a snail's pace across the road.

But when she heard a *clop-clop* sound, she froze and turned.

The boy slowed his pace, then stopped. "Hey!" he called out, pushing his hat back on his head and exposing his blond hair.

"Hi," Annabeth said. "Pretty horse."

"You can pet her."

Annabeth reached out to stroke its nose, but when the horse raised its head, she quickly pulled her hand away.

The boy laughed and she noticed his white teeth. The front two overlapped, but he had a great smile just the same. "She won't hurt you. That's just her way of saying hello."

"Oh." But Annabeth didn't try to pet her again.

"Aren't you Mrs. Harp's granddaughter from New Orleans?"

Annabeth felt nauseous when he mentioned New Orleans, as if this Forest Hill boy would know everything that happened to her there. "Rose Harp is my grandmother, but I'm not from New Orleans."

"Could have sworn someone told me that."

"I've lived on the New Orleans Westbank for a year, but that doesn't make me from there." They'd also lived in Montana two years before and Kansas eighteen months before that.

Grinning, he said, "Okay. Fine by me. You can be from wherever you want." He leaned forward and stretched out his arm toward her. "I'm Colton."

"Nice to meet you," Annabeth managed to say, briefly touching his hand. She noticed Colton's blue eyes.

"You got a name?" he asked.

Annabeth blushed. "Yes, sorry. I'm Annabeth. Annabeth Harp."

Colton laughed. "I figured that part out. The Harp part, I mean. My daddy and yours were good friends growing up. He knew your momma, too."

"Oh," she said. Her parents had married very young because her mother was pregnant with her. She wondered if Colton knew that, too.

Colton straightened in the saddle. "Well, Annabeth Harp. Lady Luck and me better head back home."

"'Bye."

He started on his way, then glanced back. "You gonna be here long?"

"A few weeks."

"Maybe I'll see you tomorrow."

Later that night she curled up in her grandfather's recliner and read "The Snow Queen," but her mind kept wandering back to Colton and his horse. She'd never ridden on a horse, though she'd sat on one once. Her parents had the picture to prove it. One of those traveling photographers with a pony took a picture of three-year-old Annabeth, wearing her Dale Evans outfit—complete with Western boots, cowboy hat, and fringed vest.

"You didn't like it much," her mother told her. Now the idea of sharing a saddle with Colton held great appeal to her. She closed her eyes, concentrating on that vision. Lady Luck galloped in slow motion. Annabeth looked great—her long hair flowing in the breeze, her body a golden bronze, and her arms surrounding Colton's waist.

So the next afternoon she settled on a towel in the front yard, listening for the sound of Lady Luck's hooves hitting the road. When she did, she raised on her elbows for a better view. This time, Colton stood on the saddle as he passed Gamma Rose's house.

"Show-off," Annabeth said under her breath, blushing as if Colton had heard her.

The screen door swung open and Ryan raced into the yard. "Wow! Did you see that? That was so cool." He took off toward the road.

Annabeth sat there, paralyzed. She felt like she'd been smacked. She'd planned to walk out to the mailbox that afternoon like she did the day before, then changed her mind because it would have been too obvious. If there was anything she'd learned from observing the popular girls, it was that to attract a boy you had to play it cool. But now Ryan was waiting at the road for Colton to make his trip back around.

When Colton did, he stopped and Annabeth could see Ryan talking to him. Then Ryan raced back to the house, letting the screen door slam behind him.

"Gamma Rose!" he yelled.

"You don't have to holler. I'm not deaf yet."

"Can I ride the horse?"

"What horse?"

Ryan pointed to Colton and Lady Luck. "That guy's horse."

Annabeth was annoyed. Ryan hadn't even bothered to ask Colton his name.

Gamma Rose walked onto the front porch and peered across the yard to the road.

"Oh, that Hopkins boy. Did he say it was okay?"

"Yes."

"Only if you ride with him *and* only for a little while. We'll be eating shortly."

But Ryan was already off the porch and halfway to the road where Colton waited.

A moment later, Annabeth saw Colton dismount Lady Luck and help her little brother onto the saddle. Then he got back on, positioning himself behind Ryan, and they rode off.

Gamma Rose came out of the house and onto the porch. "Colton. That's that boy's name. Just thought of it. I used to be good with names. That's how old age gets you, one piece at a time. Pretty soon there'll be nothing left of me. And to think I'm only forty-eight."

Annabeth stared at the road.

"Are you looking forward to school?" Gamma Rose asked.

"I guess."

"I always fancied you as the writer type."

Annabeth hardly heard her grandmother's comment. She wondered where Colton and Ryan were now.

"Do you think you'd ever want to be a writer? You write such nice letters."

"Hmm?" Annabeth turned toward Gamma Rose. "I don't know. I doubt it." All she could concentrate on this summer was planning how she would survive eighth grade.

Gamma Rose started back into the house, but stopped at the doorway and turned. "You ought to think about it. Being a writer would be a fine life."

Though it seemed like an hour, Colton and Ryan were gone about ten minutes. Annabeth knew it was ten minutes because she'd checked her watch every twenty seconds. It took a lot of restraint for Annabeth not to punch her brother silly. She hated Ryan. She should have been on Lady Luck with Colton.

Ryan was always weaseling his way into where he didn't belong.

Colton rode Lady Luck into the yard until he was just a few feet from Annabeth. She looked down, wishing she'd polished her toes with the bottle of Pink Parfait on Gamma Rose's nightstand. He helped her little brother off the horse, grinned at her, and asked, "You want to be next?"

Her heart pounded so loud, Annabeth feared Colton might be able to hear it. "No, thanks," she said, immediately wondering who on earth answered for her. She was always doing that, saying no to things when she meant yes. Or agreeing to things when she meant to say no.

Colton tipped his hat. "See you around." Then he called out to her brother, "'Bye, Cowboy."

Annabeth watched Colton ride away, her heart sinking.

"That was dumb," Ryan told her.

Annabeth agreed. Dumb, dumb, dumb.

"I would have gone again," Ryan said.

"Annabeth," Gamma Rose said, "come help set the table."

During dinner, Annabeth could think of nothing else but her stupid answer. After the meal, not even her grandmother's lemon icebox cake could make her forget the ride she'd almost had. Her face and chest felt hot.

Gamma Rose noticed, too. "You look like a crawfish. No more sun for you."

Ryan didn't help matters. All he talked about was the horse ride, spitting his words between bites of cake. He acted like they'd gone on a cattle drive to Texas instead of down the road to Butter's Cemetery and back.

He swallowed a quick gulp of milk. "And Colton made Lady Luck walk backwards. And he showed me how."

"Shut up and eat," Annabeth said.

Gamma Rose shot her a stern look. "He's just excited. Surely you can understand that?"

Annabeth wished she could understand. After dinner, she helped her grandmother do the dishes in the small kitchen. She hoped her dad would get a job soon so they could finally afford to buy a dishwasher. Her hands were starting to look chapped like those people on the television commercials before they started using Palmolive.

With the last plate put away, Annabeth filled the bathtub and poured in some bubble bath. But after testing the water with her foot, she drained some and added cold until the water became lukewarm.

She read another fairy tale while she soaked, something she knew she shouldn't do. What if she dropped the library book in the water? Tonight she didn't care. She wanted to get her mind off the afternoon, but the words on the page wouldn't sink into her head. Normally after the water cooled, she turned the left knob with her big toe, adding more hot, but tonight her skin felt sensitive and her shoulders throbbed from the sunburn.

A few minutes passed when she heard a knock at the bathroom door.

"There's a bottle of aloe vera gel in the cabinet under the sink," Gamma Rose said. "You might want to put some on before you dress."

Finally she dried off, slathered the aloe vera gel over her skin, then changed into her nightgown, and made plans for the next day. She decided she'd meet Colton at the mailbox the first time he passed by, not wait for his return trip. She didn't care if she looked obvious. And when he stopped, she'd say, "I'll take that ride now." Nothing could give her a fresh perspective like a fairy tale and a bubble bath.

The next day Annabeth watched the time and when four o'clock came around she headed outside toward the mailbox. She'd worried that Ryan would be there, too, but her grandmother's neighbor Faith

Winslow had dropped off her grandson, Sammy. He and Ryan were sprawled out on the living room floor playing Battleship.

Afraid that she'd miss Colton, Annabeth rushed to the mailbox. But when she looked down the road, no one was there. She started back toward the house, taking the tiniest steps, until she reached the half-way point. She heard a car and turned in time to see blue-haired Mrs. Lucy Cartwright drive by in her little pickup truck. She waved to Annabeth and Annabeth waved back. Finally, she went to the mail-box, opened it, and took out the mail. She walked slowly back to the house, resisting the urge to glance over her shoulder.

The next morning, she awoke to a pitter-patter sound hitting the tin roof. She looked out the window. Sheets of rain fell from the sky, but by noon it stopped and the clouds parted, making way for the sun. Hope filled up in Annabeth until four o'clock came and went with no sign of Colton.

Later, when Gamma Rose asked "How about a movie in Alex?" Annabeth agreed without hesitation. She needed the distraction.

They decided to go to the early evening movie at the MacArthur Village Cinema. *Pippi Longstocking* was playing. *The Life and Times of Judge Roy Bean*, starring Paul Newman, was playing on the other side.

"We'll have to see pretty blue eyes when it's just us girls," Gamma Rose said with a wink.

Annabeth didn't tell her that she was glad they were going to see *Pippi Longstocking*. She'd read the book when she was younger.

Ryan rode in the back with Sammy while Annabeth sat in the front seat, examining her face in the visor mirror. The sunburn had faded to dark pink, but her nose and chin had started to peel. She was thankful movie theaters were dark.

While they stood in line for the tickets, Annabeth heard a familiar voice. "Hey, Cowboy."

At the back of the line stood Colton. Annabeth took a deep breath when his eyes met hers. Now was the time to say it, she thought. Say the words she'd practiced in her head as she walked to the mailbox. *I'll take that ride now.*

But Colton spoke first. "Hey, Annabeth. Mrs. Harp. Ya'll had the same idea. Which movie are ya'll going to see?"

"*Pippi Longstocking*," Ryan said.

Annabeth thought she'd die right there in the line of the MacArthur Village Cinema.

"Are you going, too?" Ryan asked.

"No, my girlfriend twisted my arm. She's crazy for Paul Newman."

Just then a pretty, blond girl about Colton's age, wearing a halter and tight blue jeans, walked up and stood next to Colton. She was a dead ringer for Marcia Brady.

Annabeth suddenly remembered the peeling state of her face. Her hand flew to her nose. She was the ugly duckling next to the beautiful swan.

"Oh, this is Connie," Colton said.

"You're Jeffrey Albert's oldest girl, aren't you?" Gamma Rose asked.

Connie nodded. "Yes, ma'am, that's me."

She sounded as sweet as Marcia Brady, too, which made Annabeth feel even worse. It was evil to hate a sweet person. Yes, Annabeth thought. I'm an evil girl whose face is peeling like a banana.

They moved toward the front of the ticket booth and Annabeth heard Gamma Rose say, "One adult and three children for *Pippi Longstocking*."

Her first impulse was to correct her grandmother. The sign clearly stated thirteen and up were considered adults at the movies. But she knew her grandmother wasn't dishonest. Gamma Rose had just forgotten Annabeth's age for the moment. Anyway Annabeth didn't want to correct her because she realized how young thirteen would still sound to Colton and his Marcia Brady look-alike girlfriend.

They stepped inside the lobby and Gamma Rose made her way over to the concession stand. "Can't watch a movie without popcorn."

"Have fun," Colton called out to them.

Annabeth watched him from the back, his arm cradling Connie's bare shoulders as they walked toward the usher taking the tickets.

The movie seemed silly and Annabeth couldn't concentrate on it. Her mind whirled with the vision of a boy and a girl on a horse. And as much as she wanted to she couldn't squeeze Connie's face from the vision. She tried, but it wouldn't work. Connie was the girl on the horse, her long silky hair blowing in the breeze and her tan the perfect golden shade.

Later in bed, she started to read "The Princess and the Pea," but the story left her empty. She knew what was going to happen anyway. If only it ended differently, with the princess deciding she didn't want to marry the prince. Maybe then she could read to the end. But that wasn't the fairy-tale way.

A few days later, they drove over to Hilltop Baptist Church to meet the bookmobile. Ryan and Sammy were thumb wrestling in the backseat.

"Ouch!" Sammy said when Ryan bent his thumb back.

"I win! AGAIN!" shouted Ryan.

Sometimes Annabeth wished she was more like her little brother, seizing anything he wanted without thinking of consequences.

Gamma Rose glanced over at Annabeth. "I'd heard Colton's girlfriend had broken up with him a few weeks back. Didn't realize she was Jeffrey's daughter. Guess they got it all worked out."

Annabeth stayed quiet, staring through the windshield. She didn't want to pin any hope on what could have been or what could be.

A few minutes later, they climbed the steps of the bookmobile.

"Here they are again," Miss Erma said, "the book people."

Annabeth returned her book.

"Would you like another fairy tale?" Miss Erma asked. "I brought the Brothers Grimm this time."

"No, thank you." Annabeth quickly walked to the back of the bookmobile, searching for a book about a real girl without a prince.

Squealers

(1973)

THE DAY AFTER Rick Hanson's funeral, Annabeth sat in her eighth-grade social studies class, staring at his chair. She didn't know Rick well enough to call him a friend, but he sat in front of her and once even defended her. When prissy Julie Stork wouldn't lend Annabeth a pencil for a pop quiz, he'd said, "Jeez, what's the big deal? It's just a crummy pencil." That small remark had made Annabeth like him right then and there.

Rick was friendly to most, but didn't belong to anyone or any group. Every day at lunch, he leaned against the soft-drink machine on the west wall of the cafeteria, taking in the scenes around him. He looked so cool and steady as he nodded slightly at people walking by him.

The week before, some jocks hung tiny Ory Moser on the flagpole in front of the school. Students in parked buses howled as they got a close-up view of Ory dangling from his belt loop like a marionette. His face turned as flaming red as his hair. It was Rick who grabbed Ory's legs, releasing him from the flagpole. "You stupid assholes!" he'd yelled. "Don't you know how to act when you aren't holding a ball?"

When Annabeth heard Rick had drowned at Lake Pontchartrain on a fishing trip with his grandfather, she'd cried as if she'd lost a best friend, even though they'd hardly talked. There had been smiles between them. She liked the way the skin at the corners of his eyes crinkled when he grinned. She'd loved his long, curly brown hair, often resisting the urge to reach out and touch it in class. Annabeth knew deep down her feelings probably had more to do with the fact that she had no friends, unless you counted Cora Johnson, the girl in biology class she ate lunch with who kept asking her to visit the Good News Church.

The day after Rick was buried, she was daydreaming when Melody Armstrong whispered, "Did you finish your Spanish homework?"

At first she wanted to look around to see who Melody was talking to because the head cheerleader had never in her life spoken to her. "Did you?" Melody twirled a lock of her auburn hair around her finger.

"Uh, yes," Annabeth said. She had stayed up late creating sentences from that week's Spanish vocabulary. She'd never been to a funeral until that day and all her sentences were dark. *Mi hermano se ahogó en el lago.* My brother drowned at the lake. *Las señoras trajeron ropa negra al entierro.* The women wore black to the burial.

"He's in a better place," Cora had said as they lowered Rick's coffin into the ground. Annabeth had hated her for saying something so stupid.

Melody tapped her pen on the desk. She wore a mood ring that at the moment appeared amber. "Can I take a look at it?"

"My homework?"

"Mm-hm." Her lips formed a tight smile. "You don't mind, do you? I didn't have any time to do it." Then she added in a whisper, "I was at the funeral."

Obviously, Melody had not seen Annabeth there. Annabeth was tempted to mention the service ended at two o'clock, but part of her was thrilled that Melody chose her to ask of all people.

Annabeth opened her binder, then flipped through the pages, searching for the assignment. When she came to her homework, she unsnapped the rings and handed the sentences to Melody, hoping her class-mate wouldn't think she was a weirdo after she read all her depressing sentences. But Melody didn't men-tion any of them. She just hastily copied the words to a fresh sheet of paper.

The bell rang right as Melody finished. She handed the paper back to Annabeth. "Here you go." She took off for Spanish class, not bothering to ask Annabeth if she wanted to walk with her.

Annabeth's face grew hot. Letting Melody copy her homework wasn't going to win her friendship after all. And Mrs. Trulock would surely recognize the same sentences on both papers.

In class, Mrs. Trulock called roll in Spanish. The first day of school they were given Spanish names to be used in class. Annabeth's became simply Ana. It had taken her a month to respond to it, but now she didn't hesitate. In some ways she'd hoped the new name would transform her into someone different. But Ana was only said in Spanish class and Mrs. Trulock was the only one who said it.

With the roll call finished, Mrs. Trulock asked the students to hand in their homework. They passed their papers to the front of the class.

Annabeth's armpits felt sweaty. She tore off a corner from a notebook paper and rolled it into a pea-sized ball as she watched Melody pass her assignment forward, showing no guilt. She wondered if Mrs. Trulock would think Annabeth or Melody wrote the original sentences.

At lunch, Melody and her friends gathered at their table near the salad bar while Annabeth settled in her usual spot next to Cora, who was bowing her head, silently saying grace.

"Amen," Cora said aloud, then took a bite of her peanut butter sandwich. Her frizzy brown hair and big glasses overpowered her thin face. Every day she wore a blue knit cap with a button pinned to it that read "Jesus Saves." Annabeth spent most of lunch doing a mental makeover on Cora, imagining her without that ridiculous hat and her hair cut in a long shag.

"Have you made up your mind about the Bible study?" Cora asked. "Mrs. Elliot said she'd be our sponsor." She slurped her carton of milk through a skinny straw, then looked at Annabeth like she was waiting for an answer.

Annabeth couldn't believe she was asking again. "I don't want to be in a Bible study." Why couldn't she find someone else, besides Cora, to sit with at lunch? Someone who didn't think playing Twister was sinful. This year wasn't going at all as she'd planned.

"At first, it might be just the two of us," Cora said, "but I'm sure once the word gets out, there'll be more."

Annabeth stared over at Melody's table, where she was laughing with her friends. Her carefree manner annoyed Annabeth. She'd made a B+ on the first Spanish test because of late-night study sessions at the kitchen table instead of going to cheerleader practice like Melody. Annabeth was convinced that life at Marrero Junior High would have been better if she'd been a cheerleader. Then she would have had tons of friends, pearly white teeth, and be able to do a perfect split. Annabeth thought of Rick and the spunky way he snapped at Julie about the pencil. After Rick's remark, Julie had unzipped her floral pencil pouch and loaned her a yellow No. 2.

Before heading to the bus, at the end of the day, Annabeth rushed to see Mrs. Trulock. Inside the classroom, her teacher gathered her papers and slipped them into a briefcase. Annabeth tapped on the door.

"Yes? Oh, Ana, come in. Is something wrong?"

A lump gathered in Annabeth's throat and she tried to swallow.

"Yes?" Mrs. Trulock was waiting.

After taking a deep breath, Annabeth said, "I need to tell you something about my homework."

Mrs. Trulock listened patiently and when Annabeth finished, she said, "I know this was hard for you to tell me, but I'll have to mark off from your grade."

Annabeth studied the speckled linoleum floor.

"As for Miss Armstrong, I'll take care of her."

"She won't—"

"No, she won't know you told me. I'd have to be stupid to not notice the same sentences. And as you both should know, our school has a very strict policy concerning plagiarism."

Rushing to the bus, Annabeth wondered what Melody's punishment would be.

The next morning, Mrs. Trulock returned the assignments. All but one. Melody looked around as if someone else might have had her paper, then she turned in Annabeth's direction.

Annabeth's stomach sank. She glanced away. She could still feel Melody's glare.

At the end of class, Mrs. Trulock called Melody to her desk. Annabeth left the room, wondering what could happen to someone who squeals on the most popular girl in school.

By lunch, the news spread through the cafeteria like the flu. With fists beneath her chin, Cora gazed in Melody's direction. "She got a zero on her Spanish homework copying someone's paper. And—she's been suspended from performing at this week's football game."

Melody and her friends shot glares across the room to Annabeth. She tried to ignore them, concentrating on the soft-drink machine and the space next to it where Rick Hanson had stood every day.

"What's wrong?" Cora asked.

"I feel sick," Annabeth said.

When she couldn't stand it any longer, she escaped to the library. Mrs. Grant, the librarian, didn't mind if students hung out there. "Anything to get kids to read," she was famous for saying. Annabeth thought Melody and her friends would never discover her in the library. She doubted they even read.

The musty smell of old books felt comforting. She headed to her favorite corner, the paperback section, and read the titles on the spines. She liked paperbacks best because they were easy to carry and easy to hold. One title caught her eye—*The Heart Is a Lonely Hunter* by Carson McCullers. The cover revealed a girl looking up at the moon. Haunted by the image, Annabeth opened to the first page.

Just as she started to read, someone bumped her so hard the book fell from her hand. "Excuse me!" Karla, one of Melody's friends, said, but by the way she said it Annabeth knew she didn't mean it.

Annabeth bent over to pick up the book. Her fingers barely brushed the cover when another shove knocked her off course.

"*Excuse* me!" Melody said, squinting at Annabeth, who had grabbed a chair to break her fall. A second friend of Melody's, who Annabeth didn't know, joined them, and the three girls stood shoulder to shoulder, forming a fence that blocked Annabeth from moving toward the door.

Annabeth glanced toward the circulation desk.

Mrs. Grant peered over her glasses. "Can I help you girls find a book?"

"No, thanks." Melody sneered at Annabeth. Then she and her friends left the library, but not before glancing back at Annabeth with their chins held high, warning.

Annabeth's head pounded as she picked up the book and walked to the circulation desk. As she checked it out, Mrs. Grant asked, "Is everything okay?"

Annabeth nodded and left for fifth period.

At home, a letter was waiting from Gamma Rose. She dropped her books on a chair and read it in the foyer. She loved her grandmother's letters and today Rose's closing words comforted her. *I'm so proud of you.* She'd try to answer the letter before she went to bed.

Red beans were cooking in the Crock-Pot on the kitchen counter and she could smell the smoked sausage that had been added. It was amazing how food would cook in that pot without burning while they left the house. Her dad gave it to her mom for Christmas last year, but he used it now.

Annabeth grabbed a dill pickle and flopped in front of the television, watching the rest of *Another World*. She missed John Dean and his wife, Mo, at the Watergate Senate hearings. Next to visiting Gamma Rose, following the hearings had been the best part of the summer. John Dean couldn't possibly be as guilty as those other men, Annabeth thought. He had such a nice face, not extremely handsome, but he was good-looking enough to get a pretty, blond woman to marry him. Mo wasn't a ditzy blonde like some Marilyn Monroe–type. She looked sharp with her hair pulled back and dressed in suits. Annabeth would never forget the June day that she first saw them on TV. She watched John testify with Mo sitting behind him, supporting him through a hard time. They seemed so romantic. Most days, Annabeth's dad sat next to her on the couch, watching the trials.

"He's a crook, too," her dad had said about John Dean. "Only the worst kind, a squealer."

Today Merle wasn't home. Maybe he was on a job interview. When he had lost his job six months ago, her mother went to work at Sears to help make ends meet. It had been an adjustment seeing her dad instead of her mom when she walked in from school. Once she found Merle sleeping on the couch and when he awoke he'd acted guilty as if he was a little kid who'd been caught doing something wrong. She hadn't liked how that made her feel.

She missed her mom asking how her day went. Lily was a good listener. If Annabeth had a bad day, her mom knew right off. "How about some hot tea and vanilla wafers?" she'd offer. Ten minutes later she'd told her mom everything. She felt instantly better. Now Lily was always tired. Annabeth didn't want her to fret over her problems.

The house was dark, so Annabeth drew the drapes covering the sliding glass door. In the backyard, her brother, Ryan, was playing soldiers at war with his friends. For that she was relieved. With the way things had gone today she might kill him if he crossed her.

An hour later Merle walked in, dressed in gray sweats and a light jacket. He held his prized metal detector in his right hand. Gamma Rose often mentioned how as a boy he'd loved to trap wild animals. That thought repulsed Annabeth. Now Merle scouted for metal. Mostly he found dropped coins that he added to a giant pickle jar to be used for a future Disneyland trip. There had been other finds—some Mexican coins, an aluminum salt and pepper shaker set, a child's wagon handle. Sometimes Ryan went with him. Once they got excited because they thought they'd finally found something big. They were right. After digging for an hour they uncovered a Volkswagen bumper. They'd all had a good laugh at that treasure. The bumper now hung on the garage wall right next to the prized bobcat Merle had shot as a kid.

Annabeth wished he'd hurry and put away the

detector before her mother returned from work. Lily expected Merle to be on job interviews all day. Annabeth could tell she hated working at Sears. Lily wanted to be home again, cooking for the family and watching *Days of Our Lives*. These days Merle watched her soap opera. He claimed to do it to keep Lily caught up. Doug and Julie Reports, he called them. And the first few weeks, her mother clung to every word. Lately, though, he hadn't brought up the soap opera at all and her mother hadn't asked.

"Hey, Tinkerbell!" her dad said. "How was your day?"

"Fine," she lied.

"I noticed that you got a letter from Gamma Rose. What did she have to say?"

"Miss Erma got sick last week, and Gamma Rose got to drive the bookmobile. Do you want to read it?"

"No, it's your letter. I'll try and write her soon."

Annabeth knew he probably wouldn't. When he had a job they called Gamma Rose once a week. They would all take turns talking two minutes because long distance was so expensive. Annabeth enjoyed the letters best anyway.

"Your grandmother writes great letters. She used to write stories, too."

"I didn't know that."

"Yeah, you ought to ask to see one of the hundreds she wrote in those old tablets. Your granddad used to tease her that she was going to make him go broke from buying paper and pens."

Annabeth wondered if her grandmother had thrown the stories away because she'd never seen any tablets. She'd make a point to ask the next time she visited.

Merle disappeared into the kitchen to finish making dinner while Annabeth turned off the television and went upstairs to do her homework. *The Heart Is a Lonely Hunter* was on top of her textbooks. A sour feeling filled her gut, remembering the incident at the library. If only she'd thought about Melody's power to team up for revenge, she would never have told. She opened the book and began to read. An hour passed before she knew it. She already cared about each character, but most of all for Mick, a thirteen-year-old girl who wants friends.

Later Annabeth set the dinner table, placing the turquoise Fiestaware on the woven placemats. Gamma Rose gave the dishes to their family when she discovered Annabeth's mother had bought one in an antique shop. "Mercy, Lily Bea, don't pay for that," Gamma Rose had said. "I have that old stuff in a box in my closet and I've wanted to get rid of it. Heck, Merle Henry ate on those, growing up."

"Dinner is served," Merle said in a lousy attempt at a British accent. Ryan and Annabeth giggled, but Lily just rolled her eyes.

"Did anybody try to rob you today?" Ryan asked. Ever since he heard about the armed robbery at a Canal Street jewelry store, her brother thought the Sears jewelry counter at the West Oaks Mall might be next.

"No," their mother answered, smoothing a lock of frosted hair behind her ear. "But someone in my department did get fired today."

"Cathy?" Annabeth thought it must be the sixteen-year-old girl who kept forgetting to lock the jewelry cases when she closed at night.

"Yep." Lily smirked, then took a sip of iced tea. "The security manager asked me to check the cases this morning and let him know if she forgot to lock them again. Apparently they'd warned her and she's been on probation."

Annabeth couldn't help but think how her mother was a squealer, too. Maybe the trait ran in the family. Only, telling on Melody had been painful for Annabeth, and Lily almost looked pleased about helping Cathy get fired.

"Foolish girl," Lily said. "She was making good money for a kid."

Merle glanced away.

After dinner, Annabeth went for a walk in the neighborhood park, taking the book with her. A ray of light beamed through the gray clouds, and she thought of turning back but changed her mind. She settled on a bench and began to read more. She'd been reading a half hour or so when a guy walked up and asked, "How do you like that book?"

His question took her a moment to register, before she answered, "I like it."

"I read it when I was in college," he said. He was dressed in a sweater and neatly pressed pants, but he looked like he needed a shave.

Annabeth smiled.

"McCullers is great," he said. "Didn't care much for *Ballad of the Sad Café*, though."

"I haven't read that."

"Mind if I smoke?" He settled on the other end of the bench.

Annabeth shook her head. She suddenly felt sophisticated, sitting next to an older guy who was smoking and talking to her about a book. Maybe if Rick had lived, they would have started talking about books. She wondered what John and Mo Dean talked about.

"My name's Edward." He took a long drag from his cigarette and peered sideways at her.

"I'm Annabeth."

Each night after dinner, Annabeth returned to the park bench. So did Edward. Two weeks later, she knew nothing about him except that he liked Steinbeck, Camel cigarettes, and thought Hemingway was a chauvinistic ass. "He has no respect for women. That's evident in his stories. He's probably one of those men who hated his mother."

Annabeth wondered what her own mother would think if she knew that for the past couple of weeks she'd shared a park bench with an older guy. She didn't care. Knowing that she would see Edward later got her through the school day. Though when she'd think about meeting him, it wasn't Edward's face she imagined but Rick Hanson's. She thought of that image so much that she was almost startled when each night around seven o'clock it was Edward who approached her and not Rick.

She read *The Grapes of Wrath* so she'd have something to say to him that sounded smart and sophisticated, not like a thirteen-year-old. She listened carefully to everything that came from his mouth so that she could research the topics that most interested him. Now Mrs. Grant greeted her by name since Annabeth took refuge at the library every day after quickly eating lunch.

During the school day, she began to feel numb each time Melody or one of her friends gave her a dirty look. Instead, she concentrated on her new life after school at the park. By mid-October the harassment faded. Melody was too busy campaigning for homecoming court votes.

One November night, Annabeth was so wrapped up in Edward's talk about the political issues in *The Grapes of Wrath* that she didn't see Melody and her friends at the park until they'd passed by the bench. When she discovered the girls, their backs were already to her. What a close call, she thought. They hadn't noticed her. But then Melody turned her head and tossed a wicked smile Annabeth's way. A feeling of doom fell over her. What could they do? She'd done nothing wrong. She didn't hear another word Edward said that evening.

The next day at lunch, Cora had been unusually quiet. She fiddled with her cross necklace between bites. Finally she said, "God will forgive you if you ask Him."

Annabeth scowled. "What's that supposed to mean?"

Cora folded her napkin and returned it to her lunch bag. "I don't like to gossip, but I heard about you and that man."

"What man?" Annabeth asked.

"Edward Connors. His mom belongs to our church. She's always putting her son on our prayer list. You better be careful."

Annabeth studied her salad. She still didn't know much about Edward except how he felt about books and writers. But Cora's remark made him sound like a mass murderer.

"Edward came back from Vietnam two years ago, and he's never been the same. His mom said he's not stable. That's why he doesn't have a job. He just hangs out at the library all day."

Annabeth stabbed a tomato with her fork and stared hard at Cora, who had started to remind Annabeth of an old bag lady.

Cora leaned over and whispered, "You shouldn't let him do those things to you. It's not right."

Dropping her fork, Annabeth said, "I don't know

what you're talking about. We haven't done any-thing."

Cora sighed and touched Annabeth's arm. "I'll pray for you."

Annabeth pulled away, returned her lunch tray, and went to the library. By the time the last bell of the day rang, Annabeth learned that she was pregnant and that her parents were sending her to a home for unwed mothers. If the rumors about me are untrue, she thought, maybe these things about Edward are, too. But she didn't know anything about him. On the bus ride home, it was all she could think about. She decided she'd ask him somehow. If they could talk about Steinbeck and McCullers why couldn't they talk about other things?

When Annabeth came home that day, her dad was sitting on the couch dressed in a business suit.

"How was your day?" Merle asked.

"Fine. Did you have an interview?"

"Yep, a pretty good one. Who knows?" He loosened his tie and lowered the knob on the television, muting Rachel's voice on *Another World*. "Annabeth, do you have anything to tell me?"

"No. Why?"

He smiled, but his eyes looked sad. "Nothing, just a weird phone call."

"Who called?"

"They didn't say. Don't worry about it. It was probably just a prank." He patted her leg and stood. "I'm going to change clothes. Want to help me make dinner?"

"Sure."

While she chopped the carrots for the beef stew, Annabeth wanted to ask more about the phone call, but she was afraid. She wondered if Melody or one of her friends made the call. Or maybe it was Cora. But Annabeth quickly decided Cora would have left her name along with an invitation to church. How did Mo Dean handle all the pressure during John's testimony?

After dinner, it was Ryan's turn to do the dishes so Annabeth excused herself and headed toward the front door, intent on going to the park. She decided she'd ask Edward what he thought of the war as a way to open the subject.

Just as she turned the doorknob, Merle's hand covered hers. "I'd like you to stay in tonight."

"But it's Ryan's turn—"

"You don't have to do the dishes, just stay home."

And even though her dad's voice was gentle, it was also firm and she knew better than to argue. She turned away but not before noticing the metal detector in his hands as he left the house. She tried to convince herself that he was just looking for change, though she felt uneasy, waiting for his return.

Less than half an hour later, she heard someone unlocking the front door. From the den, she saw Merle put the detector away in the closet. Instead of going straight to the pickle jar in the kitchen, he went to the living room where Lily was knitting. Annabeth traced his steps through the hallway and stopped outside the living room entrance where she could hear without being seen. Soon, her mother asked, "What did you say to him, Merle?"

"I told him to leave her alone. She's thirteen years old."

"Good," Lily said.

They were quiet then except for the squeaking sound of her father settling into his vinyl recliner and the *click-click* of her mother's knitting needles.

Annabeth slowly made her way down the hall and climbed the stairs to her bedroom. She felt as if everyone were dictating her life. Later, she lay in bed and thought not of Edward or Melody or the rumors surrounding her, but of Rick Hanson. As she fought sleep, her mind drifted to the Watergate hearings. She was sitting in Mo's place, but not behind John Dean. She was sitting behind Rick, just like in social studies class. Rick leaned into the microphone. He answered the senators' questions, brave as always.

That night she did something Cora had been nagging her to do for the whole semester. She prayed. But she did not pray for forgiveness or for Jesus to come into her heart. She prayed that for just one day she could have the courage of Rick Hanson wash over her body like water in a baptism.

The next morning, Annabeth picked out her clothes. She decided on her bell-bottomed jeans and a red turtleneck Gamma Rose gave her. She rarely wore the sweater because red made her feel conspicuous. But today red was the perfect color.

At school she marched down the central hall. A small crowd hung out near her locker, their talk ceasing as they watched her approach. Annabeth yanked off the pacifier taped to the locker door, gathered her books for the first class, and walked to the cafeteria where Melody and her friends sat in a circle. When she reached their group, she threw the pacifier at Melody. It bounced off her chest and landed in her lap.

Nervous gasps and giggles scattered around their circle, but Melody just stared, wide-eyed, as if she'd never seen Annabeth in her life.

"I believe that's yours," Annabeth said. "Why

don't you try using it? It might keep you out of trouble."

Annabeth stared at Melody, holding the look for a long moment. She was tired of being pushed, teased, and lied about. The harassment might not be over yet, but one thing was for sure. She would not hide or stay silent any longer. She'd fight back even if that meant squealing. Annabeth turned on her heel, walking away with a skip in her step and Rick Hanson's courage tucked deep inside her.

Kyle

Summer Job

(2004)

ANNABETH RAPPED GENTLY on her son's bedroom door. "Wake up, Kyle, Kyle, Crocodile."

Kyle turned over. When he was five, his mother read *Lyle, Lyle, Crocodile* to him. The twist of the words had become her pet name for him, especially when she wanted him to do something like get out of bed.

Next came a loud knock. "Get up!" Paul Koami ordered. This time Kyle opened his eyes and sat. People would have thought his dad was a marine the way he barked out commands.

Kyle looked at the alarm clock: 10:13 a.m. First day of summer vacation. Can't they give a kid a break?

He swung his legs over the side of his bed and slipped on a pair of shorts he found wadded on the floor. If it weren't Saturday he could get away with no shirt downstairs, but his dad was home and Paul Koami didn't put up with sloppiness. Kyle dug in the top drawer of his chest for a Pink Floyd T-shirt, one of seven he'd bought at thrift stores. Three of them didn't fit anymore. He was thirteen years old and as big as some hefty sixteen-year-olds. His gut hung over his waistband and his legs were thick as tree trunks. Kyle suspected they had a sumo wrestler somewhere in his family's past. When he'd asked his dad, he'd said, "You'll have to talk to your grand-father. He knows more about our ancestors."

Pappy had gotten excited about his grandson's sudden interest in family history. He was a first-generation American but still took pride in his Japanese roots. "No," Pappy said, "we don't have any sumo wrestlers," then added proudly, "but three generations were thread merchants. I guess you got that belly eating too many Twinkies."

Kyle put a rubber band around his hair and went to the bathroom, peed, then splashed cold water on his face at the sink.

Downstairs everyone was dressed for the day. Kyle's slender dad wore a white button-down shirt and khakis, his I-have-to-go-into-the-office-even-though-it's-Saturday uniform. His mother and sister wore floral sundresses. He knew his mother was pretty, and everyone said Emma was beautiful. Though he liked to call her Barf-face.

He opened the frosted blueberry Pop-Tarts box and pulled out a package. Then he settled at the kitchen table across from his dad, who frowned at his T-shirt. "I didn't like Pink Floyd when they were popular," he'd said to Kyle once. When Kyle had first worn the shirt to school his friends didn't even know who Pink Floyd was and it kind of pissed him off. But that same day, two of his teachers said they thought his shirt was cool. He had paid more attention in English and world history ever since.

His dad cleared his throat. "I'm going to the office this morning, but we need to talk about something. I told you back in April, you are not spending this summer like last."

Kyle had loved last summer. He'd slept till noon or so, ate, lay on his bed listening to Led Zep or Pink Floyd or any of the other 70s groups he liked. At night he logged online and conversed in chat rooms with other hard-rock freaks. It excited Kyle to think that there were a million other people crazy about hard rock.

"Are you listening to me?" Paul snapped, waking Kyle from his daydream.

"Yes, sir."

"I found this on the door today."

Kyle looked down at the flyer his dad held out to him.

Mowing—Good Work. Reliable.
Yards: $20 and up. Flowerbeds included.
Call Michael B. Turner at 555–7046.

"Now you have competition. If you'd been as industrious as this young man, you'd already have a business lined up for the summer."

Kyle opened his blueberry Pop-Tarts package and took a bite. He knew a Mike Turner from school who was the eighth-grade vice president last year. He wondered if this was the same guy as Michael B. Turner.

"Another thing," his dad said, "you might think about cutting that hair."

Annabeth walked over and tugged at Kyle's pony-tail. "Oh, Paul, I like Kyle's hair. It reminds me of yours when I met you at LSU."

"I washed mine every once in a while, Annabeth."

Paul stood and took his plate over to the dishwasher. "Your sister works."

"Yeah, but she doesn't get paid. What kind of job is that?"

Emma scowled. "At least volunteering at the library looks good on my résumé." His sister planned to apply to all the Ivy League schools in the country. She wanted to be a doctor. Kyle could already see it—his dad at parties with his arm around Emma. "Have I introduced you to my daughter, the doctor? Oh yeah, I have a son, too. That's him in the corner with the earphones, listening to some rock crap. One of these days he's going to start a lawn service or maybe become a sumo wrestler."

Paul filled his travel mug with coffee. "You better have some work lined up by dinnertime, young man." Before leaving, he walked over to Annabeth and embraced her. His parents could be so mushy.

His mom left soon after his dad to attend a meeting. Once someone asked Kyle what his mom did for a living.

"She makes lists," he'd said. In truth, Annabeth was on about a dozen committees. Most important to her was the Algiers Point Historical Society, where she served as vice president. His mom was all about making the neighborhood look like it did two hundred years ago.

Kyle ate his Pop-Tarts slowly, thinking about what his dad had said. He really sounded serious this time.

Emma took off for the library. He listened to her old orange Volkswagen's putter fade away. The only thing cool about his sister was that car. He hoped he would inherit it when she went off to her Ivy League college.

He went upstairs to brush his teeth and practiced his pitch in the mirror. "Hi, I'm Kyle Koami, your neighbor. How about letting me mow your lawn?" Too forceful, he decided.

"Hi, Kyle Koami here. That lawn looks like it hasn't seen a lawn mower in quite a while." Kind of insulting. Oh well, he thought, I might as well just go for it.

He left the house and scoped out the street. Algiers Point was one of the oldest neighborhoods in the New Orleans area. His parents had moved there right after they married, buying one of the few camel-back houses, meaning it had half a second story. They said back then the neighborhood consisted mainly of run-down shotgun singles and doubles.

Now, almost all the colorful houses had been fixed up. Kyle liked the postage-stamp–size yards. Mowing this street ought to be a breeze, he thought. He could even do it with a Weed Eater. Of course now he'd probably have to include the flowerbeds because of Michael B. Turner.

Kyle started next door. He sure hoped Mr. Mickey had forgiven him for accidentally running over his cat when he sneaked his sister's Volkswagen out of the driveway. How was he to know that a deaf cat was sleeping with its tail under the left rear wheel? Besides, the cat had survived and looked cool with a bobbed tail.

Potted pink geraniums hung over Mr. Mickey's front porch. Kyle rang the doorbell. Mr. Mickey came to the door, newspaper tucked under his arm. He peered at Kyle over eyeglasses worn low on his nose.

"Hi, Mr. Mickey. I'm Kyle Koami, your next-door—"

"I know who you are. You're that kid who ran over Peaches."

"Well—yes, sir, that's me. I was just wondering if you had anyone lined up to mow your lawn."

"Nope, I don't. But if I do, it sure as hell won't be

you." Mr. Mickey closed the door so quickly that Kyle stood there for a moment, stung. Some people just didn't know how to forgive and forget.

Next house. Next victim. "Hi. I'm Kyle Koami, from two doors down. I was wondering if you had anyone lined up to mow your lawn this summer. I could offer you a good deal."

The woman with a messy-faced baby on her hip stared at Kyle a long moment. Kyle started to wonder if she didn't understand English. Just as he was about to tell her the baby was cute, the woman spoke. "Aren't you that boy who ran over Mr. Mickey's cat?"

Kyle decided to skip over to Vallette, the next street. But when he started to approach the corner house, he saw smooth-smiling Mike Turner strolling his way with the lawn mower. He did look more like a Michael B. Turner. Every short blond hair on his head glistened and he had the bronze skin of a life-guard. Probably a fake bake, thought Kyle. I'll bet he doesn't even sweat when he mows.

Before Michael reached the yard, Kyle pivoted and crossed the street. The next homeowner opened the door, greeting Kyle with a smile. Fishing lures decorated the man's canvas hat. A man with a weekend hobby was a good prospect. Maybe Kyle's luck was about to change.

"Hi," the man said, "I wasn't expecting you so soon. Your mom said you had a few houses to get to before mine."

Kyle looked confused and the man seemed to notice. He picked up the flyer sitting on a table in his foyer and showed Kyle. It was the same one his dad had shown him earlier. "This isn't yours, is it?"

"'Fraid not."

"Sorry, but I've already arranged to have my lawn mowed by Michael."

"No problem," Kyle said. "Thanks anyway." He turned around to leave.

The man called after him. "But if something doesn't work out, I'll let you know."

Walking down Vallette, he came to the blown glass studio where a Help Wanted sign was in the window. Kyle thought back to the time his kindergarten class took a tour there. He didn't mean to break that vase. Glass was just fragile. Kyle kept walking.

The sun, already high in the sky, beat down on him. His T-shirt stuck to his back and chest like a second skin. Maybe he should walk to the levee and get a sno-ball. Then he could kill two birds with one stone and get a job. If he worked there, he could probably have all the sno-balls he wanted.

Kyle headed toward the river. Some moms were swinging their kids at Confetti Park. He peered through the multicolored iron fence. When he was younger, he'd had a lot of good times in that park. He thought of sitting on the bench and watching the kids for a while, but when he heard the church bell chime eleven times, he kept walking. He passed Westbank Java, then stopped and turned around. An old guy sat at an iron rod table, drinking from a white cup outside the coffee shop. Inside, the shop smelled like strong espresso with a hint of cinnamon. Kyle went inside and over to the counter.

"What can I get you?" the girl with a nose ring asked.

"Who, me? I don't drink coffee. I tried it once, though. It tasted like burnt rubber. I was just wondering if you had any job openings."

Without a comment, the girl pulled two sheets from a binder on the counter. One was an application. The other was a sheet that said: PLEASE READ BEFORE FILLING OUT APPLICATION. 1. *No felons need apply.* 2. *Applicant must be at least 17 years old.* There was no reason for Kyle to read further.

"Thanks anyway," he said, then left.

A few minutes later, Kyle saw the Mr. Carmine's N'AWLINS SNO-BALLS sign. Beyond the stand, the ferry was midway in its journey across the Mississippi River. Every day his dad took the ferry to work on the east bank. Maybe there was a job waiting for him across the river, too.

At the stand, Kyle decided to take a slow approach, first coming from a customer's angle. He ordered a large blackberry sno-ball.

"Delicious," Kyle said after his first big slurp. Mr. Carmine's sno-balls were famous for their generous amount of sweet syrup.

Mr. Carmine grinned. "You ever try any other flavor? You've been ordering blackberry since you were eight years old. Once you almost ordered orange, but you changed your mind at the last minute."

Mr. Carmine sure had a great memory. That must have happened years ago.

"I just know that blackberry is always good. I'm afraid I'll miss it. But I know how I might start ordering other flavors."

"How's that?"

"Hire me for the summer. I'm sure I'll get tempted by other customers' orders."

"That's kind of an expensive way for me to get you to order something new."

"Well, actually, Mr. Carmine, I'm looking for a job."

"Sorry, kid. Why do you think I'm here? I'd have had someone else working for me long ago if I could afford it. You gotta sell a lot of sno-balls to make a living."

Next door was The Dry Dock Café and Bar, his favorite place for his favorite meal—an oyster po'-boy with a side of sweet potato fries. But he wasn't old enough to work there.

After a good-luck send-off from Mr. Carmine, Kyle decided he'd done enough job prospecting for the morning. He was getting hungry for something more substantial than a sno-ball. Walking home, he smacked a mosquito off his arm and wiped the sweat off his face. There must be a better way to make a summer living. He knew his dad would find Kyle work if he didn't have something by the end of the day. And that job probably wouldn't include air-conditioning.

At home, Kyle finished off three hot dogs, a bag of corn chips, and a Coke. He was getting sleepy. Then an idea came to him. What about working at the coolest place on earth? The Record Shop. He loved those old albums. Some were corny like Sinatra, Bing

Crosby, and Tom Jones. But Bill also had the greatest stock of 70s hard rock. Kyle dialed the number he knew by heart. "Hey, Bill. It's Kyle Koami."

"Hey, dude. What's up? Need some Hendrix? Oh, today I got a Doors in you might like."

"Cool." For a second, Kyle forgot why he'd called. "Listen, my dad is on my case about getting a job this summer."

"Bummer."

"Yeah, anyway how'd you like me to work for you?"

"Sorry, dude, no can do. I don't have the bread to hire you."

"I'm only thirteen. You wouldn't have to pay me minimum wage." Kyle would have paid Bill to work at The Record Shop if he'd had the money.

"Dude, that would be so cool, but I can barely pay my rent. If it weren't for the reefer, I'd be on the street. Hey, you didn't hear me say that. You know most people aren't like you and me. We know albums are the only way to listen to music. Most people these days want CDs. You ever thought about mowing lawns? When I was your age there was this dude that lived down the street who made a killing one summer. He put out these flyers with his name and number on it and everything. I thought about doing that, too, but it was already too late."

Kyle saw his future flash in front of him. He was standing behind the counter of The Record Shop, selling reefer to potheads. Maybe his dad was right, maybe he should cut his hair. Naah, his hair didn't have anything to do with it. He stretched out on his bed and stared at his Led Zep poster on the wall. In no time at all, he was asleep.

"Kyle, Kyle, Crocodile, wake up."

Had he slept through the entire day and evening? Opening his eyes, he realized it wasn't his mother's voice he'd heard, but his sister's. Emma stood before him. She'd inherited the best of his parents' physical traits. Kyle had to admit that with her long black hair and green eyes she was pretty enough to be a cheerleader, but Emma hated the idea of doing anything that didn't require intelligence.

"What do you want, Barf-face?" Kyle asked her. No need for her to know he thought she was pretty.

"Just for that, I don't think I'm going to tell you why I came home for lunch."

Curiosity could kill Kyle. "Okay. I take it back. Why did you come home for lunch?"

"A potential job."

"For me?"

"That's right. Mr. Patrick said he could use someone to help him with the summer skits."

"You mean I'd have to wear costumes and silly wigs?" He remembered when he was little and Mr. Patrick wore a long wig with antlers for a Christmas skit based on the book *Imogene's Antlers*. It was a scary sight.

"Yep, exactly. But it should be fun."

"No way."

"Fine." Emma left his room.

He'd expected a bigger fight than that. He *needed* a bigger fight than that. What was with Barf-face anyway? She never gave up that easily. Still, he had to admit he was amazed that she would tell him about a job that would mean she'd have to work with him. A little brother who called her Barf-face.

He went downstairs, where she was making a ham sandwich.

"I guess all these skits will be based on books, right?"

Emma made a snapping noise with her tongue. "Well, it is a library."

"Hmm. Figures." Kyle hated to read. He was the only one in the family who did. It had perplexed him how his mom would forget to make dinner because she was engrossed in *Confessions of an Ugly Stepsister*. Or how his dad could find fascination in yet one more WWII book. How much could someone read about WWII anyway? And Emma was famous for reading. She always had a book in her hands. The only stories he'd enjoyed were the ones Gamma Rose made up and read to him. He loved the adventures of Alligator Man on the bayou. When she'd read those to him, she used a Cajun accent. "My momma used to talk that way," she'd say. She also usually fed him a bowl of gumbo when she was finished. Maybe it was the gumbo he'd liked, not the stories. The idea of being surrounded by books every day at the library caused Kyle to shudder. Still, it was a job, a job with air-conditioning.

He waited for Emma to say something, but she just ate in silence, skimming an article in *Psychology Today*. Then she went upstairs for a minute before taking off. From the living room window, Kyle watched the VW drive down the street and disappear around the corner.

Upstairs, he checked the Pink Floyd chat room to see if JJ had logged on. JJ usually didn't show up until the evening and nobody was saying anything new. He put on a Led Zeppelin album and turned up the volume loud enough to make his dad yell if he'd been home, but not loud enough to cause Mr. Mickey to call the cops. The posters on his wall vibrated. For a moment it satisfied him. Then he lowered the volume.

A lawn mower roared somewhere in the distance, probably Michael B. Turner raking in more cash. Peeking between his blinds, he noticed Peaches curled up on top of the empty birdbath in Mr. Mickey's backyard. That sure was a lazy cat. Getting run over was probably the most exciting thing that ever happened in her life. Kyle thought about last summer. He dragged the phonebook from under his bed and searched for the Algiers Public Library's number. With "Stairway to Heaven" softly playing in the background, he heard himself say, "Mr. Patrick, this is Kyle Koami. Emma said you might have a job for me."

Missing Harry

(2004)

IT WAS FRIDAY, the last day for *Turnip Soup*. Kyle had performed in skits at the Algiers Public Library all summer. Each weekday became a routine. He hated getting up early, but after that the day wasn't so bad. He had liked some of the skits, even if they were based on books.

Kyle's first day on the job, Mr. Patrick had asked him, "Have you read *Squash Pie*?"

"Nope," Kyle answered.

"How about *The Wolf's Chicken Stew*?"

"'Fraid not."

"What kind of books do you like to read?"

"Ummm . . . do you have any books on the Stones?"

"You mean like rocks?" Mr. Patrick asked.

"No. The Rolling Stones. Or maybe one on Hendrix or Pink Floyd."

Mr. Patrick looked a bit taken aback. Kyle thought he was probably wondering how he could be related to his sister, Emma. But after a short pause, Mr. Patrick told him where to find the biographies downstairs in nonfiction. Six weeks later, Kyle still hadn't bothered to look for the books. He could find anything he wanted to know online.

Since they did a morning skit and an early afternoon show, he had to hang out at the library until his sister got off work. At least he was earning cold cash.

He couldn't wait for tomorrow. Every Saturday he talked his mom into driving him to The Record Shop across the river. Since the store was near Magazine Street she didn't mind. She would browse the antique shops while Kyle looked for an album to add to his collection.

Now he and Emma rode to the library in silence. Neither one of them was a morning person like their mom. Kyle leaned over and turned on the radio, tuning to his favorite station. He'd barely recognized the song when Emma switched to NPR.

"Hey."

"Hey, my car."

Kyle didn't feel like arguing. He just leaned his head against the window while *Morning Edition* droned on. No wonder his sister was so smart, if she liked listening to this crap.

They drove until they reached the library parking lot, then got out and walked past the homeless people lingering outside, waiting for the library to open. Emma always looked at the ground when she passed them, as if they were invisible, but Kyle looked them straight in the eyes and said, "Hey. How's it going?" Usually he got a nod, sometimes a "Good morning."

Kyle wondered what had happened to make them homeless. Did they get fired? Did they lose their entire family in some tragedy? He tried to memorize their faces like a camera taking photos. The woman with the plaid jacket and long denim skirt reminded him of his fifth-grade teacher. At first he thought it was her, but then she grinned and he noticed she didn't have any teeth. Mrs. O'Brien had long donkey-sized ones. Kyle thought the bald man with Elvis sideburns had kind eyes. Another man was almost as small as a child. He always wore a tweed jacket and a knit cap with earflaps, even though it was in the middle of the summer.

Upstairs in the youth section, Kyle helped Ms. Carol find Web sites for kids until the morning skit started. To his disappointment, none of them asked to see any hard-rock sites. They never did. They all seemed interested in subjects like gemstones and dinosaurs.

That morning, Mr. Patrick walked in with a book. Kyle averted his eyes, staring back at the monitor where he was helping a little girl find sites on butterflies. He hoped Mr. Patrick wasn't going to do what he did almost every day. Mr. Patrick would say, "Let me give you a short book talk on this great story." Then he proceeded to give Kyle a synopsis of a young-adult novel with such excitement that Kyle clapped at the ending. But he never checked out the book. The only books Kyle had read that summer were the picture books that inspired the skits, and that was only because he had to understand how to act out his role.

Glancing up from the monitor, Kyle was relieved when Mr. Patrick placed the book on Ms. Carol's desk. He noticed the book was a Harry Potter one.

Mr. Patrick sighed. "The replacement arrived, but there's another one missing from the stacks."

"Again?" Ms. Carol asked.

"Yep."

Kyle kept listening while he clicked on a Web site about butterflies in Africa.

"At least they're consistent," Mr. Patrick said. "Another Harry Potter."

"A Harry Potter book is missing?" Kyle asked. Most of his friends had claimed to have read all of them. He'd just brushed it off as a fad.

Kyle was standing now. "Do you think somebody stole it?"

"Well, maybe," Mr. Patrick said.

"Probably," Ms. Carol said, shaking her head. "That's the second one."

Kyle found this robbery talk fascinating. Imagine, a mystery right here in Algiers Public Library. "That means the thief is probably the same kid."

Emma, who was shelving picture books, looked their way. "That's right, Detective Koami."

Kyle gave her a you-better-not glare, but Emma just winked. When Kyle was seven, his teacher read *Encyclopedia Brown* to the class. He was so inspired that he started his own detective agency. He even posted a sign. MYSTERIES SOLVED—25 CENTS. CALL KYLE KOAMI, BOY DETECTIVE. His mother gave him twenty-five cents for finding any of her shoes she was always misplacing, but Kyle had yearned for a real mystery to solve. For days, he spied on their neighbor Mr. Mickey with binoculars. The weirdest thing he did, though, was shake pepper on his roses.

"Almost show time," Mr. Patrick announced, shelving *Harry Potter and the Chamber of Secrets* with the other Harry Potter books. Mr. Patrick got so caught up when it was time for a skit. He'd already forgotten his plan to keep the new Harry Potter books on Ms. Carol's desk.

Ms. Carol had forgotten, too. Her heels clicked against the floor as she rushed to the bathroom to change into her costume.

Kyle didn't mention the oversight because he decided the book would make great bait. He watched the P–T section where the Harry Potter books were shelved while the kids poured into the Story Time room. Right away, a girl went over to search the shelf and began bouncing on her toes when she saw *Harry Potter and the Chamber of Secrets* among the three first Harry Potters.

"Cool!" she said and pulled it from the shelf.

Kyle followed her until she met up with her mom standing at the circulation desk. There went the bait, thought Kyle. That girl lucked out, too, because Ms. Carol kept a list of names of people waiting for the next book in the series.

Kyle couldn't imagine any book good enough to

be on some waiting list. No book could match getting a Jimi Hendrix album. Bill at The Record Shop should start a waiting list for certain in-demand titles. He could think of several times he'd asked Bill for Hendrix's *Are You Experienced?* and Bill had said, "Sorry, dude, just sold it." If Bill kept a list, Kyle could be the first to sign up. But Bill wasn't a list kind of person. So scratch that idea.

After the last *Turnip Soup* performance, Kyle noticed a red-headed kid he'd seen the day before, but hadn't given him much thought until now. The boy wandered around the youth section, never looking at any books, always waiting for another turn on the computer. Or maybe, Kyle thought, he was just pretending to wait for it. Maybe he was really waiting for the coast to be clear when he'd go in for the big steal.

Mr. Patrick held up a white cowboy hat and a black one. "Bad guy or good guy?"

"Huh?"

"Do you want to be the bad guy or the good guy? We're performing *Saving Sweetness* next week, and there's a bad guy and a good guy. There's also Sweetness, but I didn't think you'd want to play a little girl."

"That's for sure."

"The bad guy's part is a lot smaller."

"Bad guy," Kyle answered, keeping an eye on the red-headed boy.

Mr. Patrick smiled. "I thought you'd say that. Are you familiar with the story?"

"Nope."

"Well, here's the book. Take it home over the weekend and read it. I think you'll get the idea."

Kyle had had similar assignments from Mr. Patrick all summer. He'd read *Turnip Soup*, *Squash Pie*, and *The Wolf's Chicken Stew*. But those were quick reads since they were picture books. Now he was curious about that Harry Potter book. Maybe he could read just enough to get a clue. Maybe a clue hidden in the book would lead him to why some kid was stealing them. If he was lucky, maybe he'd find the clue on page one. If there was anything his days as a detective had taught him it was to keep an open mind. You never knew where you'd find a clue. So when Ms. Carol started to place another *Harry Potter and the Sorcerer's Stone* on the shelf, he asked, "Can I check that out?"

On the ride back home, Emma said, "You checked out *Harry Potter*?"

"Yeah. Have you read it?"

"A few years ago."

Figures, Kyle thought. "Did you like it?"

"It was okay. I don't think it lived up to the hype."

His sister often talked about the manipulation of people's minds because of marketing ploys. Never mind that their dad made a living as an advertising executive.

At home, Kyle quickly read *Saving Sweetness*. Sweetness and the good guy may have had the biggest parts, but the best part definitely belonged to the bad guy.

Dinner at the Koamis' house always included a how-was-your-day routine. His mother had started that a year ago when they got so busy with their own schedules that dinner had become a fend-for-yourself affair.

"Enough!" Annabeth announced one night as Kyle's dad came in at eight o'clock, followed by Emma, who was back from a debate team meeting. "Dinner," his mother stated, "will be at 6:30 every night, and every-one's presence is required. No exceptions."

Tonight Kyle had just taken his first bite of red beans and rice when Annabeth asked him, "How was your day?"

"Fine," Kyle said with his mouth full.

Emma dropped her fork on the plate. "Kyle checked out a book today."

Kyle thought of kicking her under the table.

"You did?" Annabeth looked as if she'd been told the historical society had been given a huge grant. "What's the title?"

"*Harry Potter and the Sorcerer's Stone,*" Kyle mumbled.

Paul nodded, smiling. "Ah, the result of a good marketing campaign."

"That's what I said," chimed Emma, not meaning the admirable way that her dad had meant.

"Well," Annabeth said, "I think it's great that you're reading, no matter what book you chose."

Kyle was tempted to say, I'm not really reading it. I'm looking for a clue. But he didn't want anyone to bring up the detective agency subject again.

Annabeth folded her napkin and placed it beside her plate. "Well, I have some news."

"What?" Emma asked.

"I received a letter from Gamma Rose today and she said she had a surprise for the family. She asked that we block off the last weekend in September."

Another mystery, thought Kyle. But this one couldn't be that interesting. This involved his great-grandmother.

Emma leaned forward. "I wonder what that's about."

"I don't know," Annabeth said, "but Mother seems to. She called today and told me that she'd tell me all about it tomorrow when she had more time. Her bridge club was about to show up. I said, 'Mother, you can't leave me hanging. Give me something.' She said it had to do with a bookmobile. Then she hung up."

A bookmobile? Now Kyle knew it wouldn't be interesting.

Paul chuckled. "Sounds like she still left you hanging."

"Didn't she used to drive a bookmobile?" Emma asked.

Annabeth nodded. "A long time ago."

"Well," said Kyle, "if she's going to drive it again, let me know so I can stay off *that* road."

Emma laughed. "You should talk. You couldn't make it out of the driveway."

Annabeth sighed. "I guess we'll have to wait until tomorrow to find out about the surprise."

Kyle decided he could wait. After dinner, he climbed the stairs and logged on as Swampman in the hard-rock chat room. He placed the Harry Potter book in his lap until JJ appeared. They met online in that chat room a few months ago and had made it a habit to check in with each other every night around 7:30 p.m.

C.W. and Earthchild were logged on, and a few others that Kyle didn't recognize. But no JJ. So Kyle opened *Harry Potter* and began to read. He'd planned to read only a page, then check in for JJ. If he wasn't there he'd move on to the next page. Before he knew it, though, he was on page twelve. He panicked when he realized how much time had passed. Looking up at the screen, he scrolled back until he saw some chatter from JJ.

JJ: Hey Swampman, you there?

JJ: Swampman?

C.W.: Haven't heard from him tonight.

Earthchild: No Swampman here.

Orange Jell-O: He hasn't been around all night.

Kyle had never heard of Orange Jell-O and for some reason it ticked him off that Orange Jell-O would try to speak about him as if they were big buds.

JJ: Well, I'm out of here. I'm going to the Star Trek movie fest that they're having downtown.

Surprisingly, Kyle didn't feel disappointed at all. He loved talking to JJ. He knew more about Pink Floyd than anyone. But Kyle returned to the book, this time reading stretched out across his bed.

He awoke with his face between pages eighty and eighty-one. *Harry Potter* was good reading, but it made for a lousy pillow. His neck ached, though it didn't stop Kyle from continuing. Like a bear, he hibernated in his room, only coming out to eat and to use the bathroom.

He didn't want his family to know what he was doing. They had made such a big deal over the book at dinner. And Kyle didn't want them fussing over the idea of him reading. Although in some ways it would be a refreshing change to hear his dad say something positive about him. Paul Koami seemed certain that his only son was destined for a life of desolation. His mom didn't treat him like that, but she kind of babied him. Even though he was dying to discuss the book, he decided to keep it to himself.

Behind closed doors, he played a Pink Floyd album, put on his earphones, but unplugged them from the stereo, to muffle the sound. He wanted to hear the words in the book. They were taking him to a new world.

Monday morning, Kyle and Emma rode in silence to work as usual until Emma asked, "How'd you like the book?"

"It was all right," Kyle said. Then he remembered his sister's review, and he risked it all, saying, "Actually, I thought it was pretty damn good."

Emma nearly drove through the stop sign. She slammed the brakes so hard, the wheels screeched, and Kyle said, "Cool. I didn't know you had it in you."

Kyle knew it wasn't the cuss word that unnerved her. She'd heard him cuss before. But she wasn't used to him saying anything great about any book. The rest of the way there, Emma stole side glances at Kyle as if he were an alien that took over her brother's body.

The red-headed kid was already at the library, using the first thirty-minute computer session. Kyle kept an eye on him until it was time for his debut as the bad guy.

Saving Sweetness proved to be Kyle's favorite skit. He loved the kids booing him. And since he finished first, Kyle left the Story Time room and went to see if *Harry Potter and the Chamber of Secrets* was in. Even Janna from Genealogy had sneaked into the Story Time room to watch the rest of the skit.

The youth section was empty of people except for the homeless man with Elvis sideburns, looking at the new YA book section. Then Kyle noticed the red-headed kid leaning over Ms. Carol's desk.

Kyle hid behind one of the bookshelves, peering through the space above the books. His heart pounded. Muffled laughter came from behind the closed Story Time room door. Kyle thought he should probably be there, too, but he'd return for the bow at the end. Besides he was about to solve the mystery of the missing Harrys.

When the boy inched over, Kyle noticed the Harry Potter book on the desk. He couldn't tell which one, but he could swear the kid was eyeing it. Suddenly a woman said, "Cody?"

The boy jumped.

"You were supposed to check in with me downstairs. Some of the newspapers hadn't arrived. Let's go home for lunch and then we can come back."

"Do I have to come back?" the kid asked.

"Yes, I'm not leaving you home by yourself. And I have to finish reading the want ads. You can read a book while I'm downstairs."

The boy groaned.

"Come on, let's go."

Kyle started to wonder if the red-headed kid was the wrong suspect. Maybe he was like Kyle and didn't enjoy reading. Or maybe he was pretending that he didn't like to read, and he really wanted to snatch that Harry Potter book. His mom had returned before he had a chance to steal it.

Kyle started to leave his hiding place when he noticed the homeless man move toward Ms. Carol's desk. Holding his breath, Kyle watched him.

The man dug inside his tattered bag and pulled out a Harry Potter book. He placed *Harry Potter and the Chamber of Secrets* on the desk. Then he slipped *Harry Potter and the Prisoner of Azkaban* inside his bag, turned, and walked away. He didn't walk fast. He sauntered, stopping to look at the rotating paperback display. A moment later, he headed downstairs.

Kyle hurried to the elevator and pushed the button. He was surprised when it opened immediately. After stepping inside, he pushed the first-floor button. His heart pounded against his chest. *Thr-ump, thr-ump, thr-ump.* The door opened. He rushed out, running smack into the homeless man. Kyle gasped, but the man merely muttered "Excuse me" and kept moving. He passed the reference desk and the periodical section.

It took Kyle a moment to catch his breath. From the periodical area, he watched the man walk to a back corner and sit at a table. The man put his bag in front of him, hiding the book before he began to read.

Kyle wished he could stay and watch him to see what would happen next, but he knew Mr. Patrick would be wondering about his whereabouts. He'd forgotten to return to take his bow at the end of the skit. He'd forgotten everything because of a book.

Finally, he had to leave. His sister was the type to overreact. She might call the police, or worse, make an announcement over the loudspeaker. The only time the library did that was for hurricane warnings. Besides, the man was so engrossed in the story, he'd surely be at the same place when Kyle returned after a while. Kyle took the stairs two at a time, and when he reached the top, Mr. Patrick was there.

"Hey, where were you? You missed the standing ovation."

For some reason, Kyle didn't tell Mr. Patrick about the man. He just shrugged. "Sorry." Then he quickly added, "We got a standing ovation?"

"Yep," Mr. Patrick said. "All the kids wanted to know where you were. We told them you were in jail."

Emma smiled at him and almost startled Kyle. It was a kind of smile Kyle hadn't seen from her in a long time—an I'm-not-embarrassed-that-I'm-related-to-you smile.

"You were great," she said. "How about lunch? We could go to The Dry Dock Café. I'll even treat."

Kyle's stomach was grumbling, but he wanted to watch the man until the next skit. "Um, I'm not so hungry." Kyle had never said those words in his entire life.

Emma's forehead wrinkled. "Suit yourself." Then she left with Carmel, one of the library aides.

Kyle returned to his watch post in the periodical section, but his stomach sank when he realized the man was gone. He circled the first floor so many times that one of the research librarians frowned and started watching him with a suspicious glare. Finally, Kyle gave up and returned to the children's area.

The only thing that made him feel better was *Harry Potter and the Chamber of Secrets*, the one the homeless man returned. Kyle grabbed it off the desk. "Ms. Carol, could you hold on to this? I'm going to check it out at the end of the day."

"Sure." She took the book from him. "Wait a minute. Where did this come from?"

"Your desk."

"This is the one that went missing the other day. Strange."

She looked frantically around and underneath her desk, again. "And now the third one is missing. The oddest things happen in this library. Just the other day someone returned a book. They'd been using a piece of bacon for a bookmark." Shaking her head, she started to put the book in her desk drawer. "Oh, Kyle, I'm sorry, but I forgot there are three other people on the waiting list for that book."

Kyle nodded, disappointed.

Ms. Carol leaned over her desk and lowered her voice. "Do you think you could finish it by Friday?"

"You bet!" Kyle sounded more excited than he'd meant to.

She winked. "It'll be right here."

Kyle wandered into the break room and ate lunch from the vending machines. It wasn't an oyster po'-boy, but in a fix two Snickers bars and a Coke could hit the spot. Then he moseyed downstairs, wishing the man would return.

The case was solved. The man wasn't a thief. Emma had recently told Kyle that the homeless couldn't check out books because people had to have an address to get a library card.

Now Kyle was just curious about him. It would be cool to strike up a conversation with the man about Harry, like he and JJ did in the chat room when they shared info on Hendrix or Zeppelin. He scoped the back section of the library. The man wasn't there.

Kyle walked over to where the man had sat and

settled into his chair. He tried to see the world from the man's eyes. He surveyed the shelves. A library must be a candy store to someone who loves to read. His gaze settled on a familiar book spine on the fourth shelf. Most people would have to use a stool to reach that shelf, but Kyle wouldn't. Sometimes being the tallest kid in middle school came in handy.

He got up and went over to the Harry Potter book that was between *The History of Philosophy* and *Questions in Philosophy*. He walked away, leaving the book on the shelf. Even though they didn't get to talk, Kyle thought of how he'd probably be reading about Harry tonight, but the man with Elvis side-burns couldn't because the library would be closed.

Kyle reached the stairs as the Sunshine Day Care Center's bus drove up in front of the library—*Saving Sweetness*'s next audience. He hoped they booed him like the morning kids.

On the second floor, Mr. Patrick looked up from behind his desk. "There you are. You're quite the mystery man, Kyle. You show up just in time, just like those missing Harry Potter books."

Kyle grinned. He looked over to Ms. Carol, who was helping a lady with a toddler find a book. Cody, the red-headed kid, was back, hovering over a boy searching the Internet.

"Excuse me, Mr. Patrick," Kyle said. "I'll be right back."

Mr. Patrick peered over his glasses. "You aren't going to do another disappearing act, are you? The kids will be seated any second now."

Kyle could hear them already climbing the stairs. "I promise. This will only take a couple of minutes."

He went to the R section and grabbed the only remaining *Harry Potter and the Sorcerer's Stone* off the shelf. He walked over to Cody, who was still watching the other boy at the computer.

"Hey," Kyle said.

"Hi," Cody murmured.

"Do you like to read?"

The boy shrugged.

"Ever read about Harry?" Kyle asked, showing Cody the book.

"No. I've seen the movie, though."

"Oh, the book is much better. Let me give you a short book talk."

Cody's mother came up just as Kyle finished his spiel. "I'm finished," she said. "Do you want to go home?"

"Yeah."

Kyle held out the book. "Don't forget this."

"You picked out a book?" Cody's mother sounded pleased.

The boy looked reluctant, but took the book from Kyle anyway. *Just wait*, Kyle thought. He watched the boy walk away with his mom, the book tucked under his arm. Kyle felt like his chest was going to burst.

When he turned, he discovered Mr. Patrick was already wearing the white cowboy hat. He held out the black one to Kyle. "Ready to play the bad guy?"

Kyle accepted the hat and placed it in on his head. "Ready."

Rose

Been Down That Road

(2004)

THE GLENMORA BRANCH of the Rapides Parish Library had never looked so festive. The room was small, but the staff managed to squeeze a long table between two rows of bookshelves. They covered it with a white linen tablecloth and, in the center, set a cookie platter next to a punch bowl filled with pink lemonade and a floating fruit ice ring. Rose's books were stacked at both ends with the top one displaying *Books on the Bayous*. It showed a photograph of a young Rose, standing near the bookmobile she'd driven years ago.

Twenty minutes remained before the afternoon reception started. The librarian Hilda Monroe and her aides were putting out a few folding chairs. Rose stood in front of the table, trying to take it all in. She wore a yellow dress, instead of the drab gray suit she'd almost chosen, because Luther had always said she looked like walking sunshine whenever she'd worn the color. If only Luther could be here today, thought Rose, then the day would be perfect.

Rose had not done everything she'd wanted to in life. She'd not gone to college, not even finished high school. Instead she'd worked to help support her family, married young, raised three children. Now at seventy-nine years old, she'd finally realized a dream come true. She'd become a writer. The book wasn't any of the stories she'd written in the Indian Chief pads or spiral notebooks. This tale told about her days as a young bookmobile driver in the bayou communities of Houma.

The book would never have happened if it wasn't for the article she submitted to *Sweet Memories* magazine. Who would have thought the story Rose wrote on a whim would find its way to the hands of a New York editor? And had the grandmother of that young editor not shared the article with her grand-daughter, Rose's book would never have existed.

The editor's letter arrived on a warm autumn morning. Rose had just finished hanging sheets on the clothesline. She owned a dryer but loved the smell of bedding that had spent the day in fresh air. Later she walked to the mailbox, returned to the house, and settled into her chair with a cup of coffee. Thumbing through the envelopes, she felt disappointed not to receive a letter from any of her family. Except for Annabeth, no one wrote letters anymore. Everyone e-mailed, whatever the heck that was. Merle Henry told her she needed a computer so they could keep in touch. "Hogwash!" she'd said.

That morning, she'd almost set the New York letter aside, mistaking it for junk mail. But she gave the envelope another look because it was addressed to Rose McGee Harp. No one had attached her name to McGee in decades. She shook her head, trying to erase the bitter feeling that surfaced every time she thought of how her father had abandoned them and how her mother had to work for years at the Boudreaux Oyster Company just to make ends meet. The only good thing that had come from her papa leaving was finally meeting her grandfather. Not long after they moved to Houma, Antoine's heart softened toward them all. When she married Luther, she told her grandfather the truth about her age. A look of relief washed over him, but it had quickly changed to horror. "You only sixteen and you marry dis man? You just a baby!"

Rose slid the letter opener under the envelope's edge and took out the page.

> *Dear Mrs. Harp,*
>
> *My grandmother sent me a copy of your article that appeared in* Sweet Memories *magazine. I was moved by your story about your days as a young bookmobile driver in 1940. Do you have more stories about this time in your life? If you do, I would like you to consider writing a book on your experiences. You have a lovely spare voice that would appeal to readers. And you capture a time and a place that many people find fascinating. Please contact me at your earliest convenience.*
>
> *Sincerely,*
> *Amelia Peters*

Rose sat there stunned, not moving an inch. Then she tried to grab the phone so quick she missed her aim, knocking it to the floor. After picking it up, she dialed the first call she'd ever made to New York City. Initially, Amelia seemed like she was too busy to talk until she'd figured out that the caller was the woman to whom she'd sent a letter.

"Oh, Mrs. Harp. How nice to hear from you."

"You really want me to write a book?"

"I'd love for you to try."

"Mercy," Rose whispered under her breath.

"Pardon?"

"How much would this cost me?" Rose asked. Her house was paid for, but she was living on Social Security and a few CDs.

"Mrs. Harp, you don't pay us. We pay you."

"Mercy," said Rose.

After the phone call, Rose dug out the leather journal she'd kept in Houma and began to write. When she completed the first draft, she cashed in a CD and bought a computer. She told no one about the book, afraid that the deal might fall through. Each morning she sat at the kitchen table and wrote about the people of Bayou du Large, Pointe-Aux-Chenes, and the other bayou communities. The spurt of energy she felt upon waking surprised her. Writing a book was better than a shot of cortisone. She could hardly feel those old aches and pains. A few months later she sent in her manuscript, thinking she'd said all she had to say about those days.

Several weeks had passed when a package arrived from Amelia Peters. It contained a seven-page letter and her manuscript. She's changed her mind, thought Rose, thankful she hadn't told anybody. Then Rose read the letter. The first page touted all the wonderful sensory details Rose used to paint a picture of life in Houma. But the following pages contained suggestions about how she thought Rose could improve the story. Amelia's last comments summed it all up. "Surely a fourteen-year-old girl experienced emotions of all sorts. How did you feel about your mother making you quit school and asking you to lie about your age? Did you have a love interest? I urge you to revisit those experiences and share them with readers."

Rose had to chew on that a bit. She didn't want to feel like she was betraying anyone she cared about. But she wanted this book to happen more than anything. Otherwise her stories would exist only in paper tablets that would probably be thrown out after she died. So a few weeks after the letter arrived, Rose opened a private place inside her and wrote about her mother, Antoine, Pie, Possum, Luther, and young Gordie.

Rose was retracing all this in the library when she felt a hand on her shoulder.

"Momma."

She glanced up, startled, because Gordie looked so much like Luther had a few years before he'd died—the deeply lined forehead, the silver hair, those eyes. Luther's blue eyes had made her grow weak until the day he drew his last breath.

Rose hugged Gordie. "Thanks for being here." She'd never formally adopted him, but he was hers.

Gordie smiled, nodding. The quiet boy had grown into a quiet man who had recently retired from being a research librarian at LSU. Rose was proud that at least one of her children had worked with words. He knew something about everything. Except maybe women. He was sixty-six years old and was finally getting married, mainly because the woman had asked *him*.

"None of us would have missed this day for the world," Merle Henry said with a wink. Lily Bea stood beside him. They'd struggled over the years with Merle Henry's wanderlust, changing jobs and cities. It was like his desire as a boy to trap a mink, thought Rose. He was never satisfied with possums or raccoons. Somehow he and Lily Bea had made it in spite of all those moves.

Rose glanced toward the door and noticed Anna-beth and her family walking in. Emma was as pretty as her mother, but she wished Kyle would cut his hair. He had such a nice face.

Rose embraced each of them. Kyle gave her a quick hug before heading toward the punch bowl and the cookie platter, even though no one else had touched the refreshments.

"Hold on, Kyle," Paul said. "They're not serving yet."

"As a matter of fact," said Rose, "my throat was starting to get dry." She joined Kyle at the punch bowl. To her surprise, Kyle filled a cup and handed it to her.

"Thank you, young man."

"Gamma Rose, is your book about Alligator Man?"

Rose nearly choked on her drink. "You remember him?"

"Of course. I remember all about him. I remember how he lived in Bayou Blue and how he rescued the fishermen and those librarians that drove around in that little bus."

Rose smiled. "The bookmobile."

"Yeah. Those were cool stories."

"I'm afraid that's not what this book is about. This one is a true story."

"Oh," Kyle said, disappointed. "Well, maybe your next book could be about Alligator Man."

Rose laughed. "Maybe so."

Now people from the community entered the library. Rose's daughter, Marie, wasn't there yet. She was late coming into this world and had never been on time a day in her life. Her carefree manner reminded Rose so much of Pie, who had just arrived wearing the most enormous pink hat she'd ever seen. It was a good thing her current boyfriend was short. He fit right under the brim of Pie's hat. Rose tried to remember his name. She knew he had been a banker. Her sister had gone through three divorces before declaring, "Marriage is like spinach. It's just not for me."

Suddenly she heard someone holler, "Rose Harp, if you aren't a sight for old eyes." Erma was being wheeled into the room by a young man, probably one of her great-grandnephews.

Rose felt a twinge of guilt. She'd visited Erma only once since Erma moved into the nursing home in Alexandria.

"I'm so proud of you, Rose. All those years around books, and I thought I'd never know a real author. All along, one was right under my nose."

Hilda stepped forward. "Could you say a few words, Mrs. Harp?"

A lump formed in Rose's throat. She'd not planned on that. But there they all were—her loved ones standing before her. She didn't know how she'd be able to speak without breaking. Just then Marie burst into the room, announcing, "Sorry! Sorry!"

Merle Henry hollered, "You're right on time, Marie. *Your* time, ten minutes late."

Everyone laughed. The moment had lightened the mood, and Rose gathered the strength she needed to carry her through.

After swallowing a sip of lemonade, Rose took a deep breath. "Seeing each of you makes me realize what a great life I've truly had just because you've been a part of it." She looked toward Erma. "Thank you for celebrating with me." Then facing her children, grandchildren, and great grandchildren, she said, "My family, you are my home."

Rose couldn't speak anymore. She felt too full. Everyone seemed to feel the same way, and for a long moment, silence fell upon the room. The afternoon train whistled outside the window and a few cars could be heard driving by.

Suddenly, Kyle yelled, "Hear, hear!" holding up his cup.

Paul shot a stern look Kyle's way, but Merle Henry rested his hands on Kyle's shoulders and said,

"Hear, hear!" And since no one had a cup except for Kyle and Rose, everyone else began to clap.

After Rose had settled behind the corner table, they all lined up to get a signed copy of *Books on the Bayous*. She wrote her name until Kyle, the last person in line, had gotten his book signed.

"Thanks, Gamma Rose. I might even read this."

Her hand throbbed, but it was a good ache. She certainly wasn't going to complain.

"Have you seen what's outside yet, Rose?" Erma asked with the same enthusiasm she'd shown years ago, putting books and people together. She looked like she was about to jump out of that wheelchair.

Everyone headed out of the cramped library and into the parking lot where Annabeth stood by her SUV.

Rose looked confused. Then Merle Henry said, "Annabeth is going to take you on your book tour, Momma."

"A book tour?" The words came out in a screech.

Annabeth stepped forward. "I hope you don't mind, Gamma Rose. I booked you at libraries from here to Houma. Here's your schedule." She handed the paper to Rose.

Rose stared down at the itinerary. All the details were there—the library talks, the hotels, when to eat.

Annabeth had scheduled everything, including a stop in Terrebonne Parish, where it had all started.

"Mother even packed your suitcase for you," said Annabeth.

Sure enough, Rose's suitcase was at Lily Bea's feet. "We knew if we told you ahead of time you wouldn't go."

Rose studied all the faces, thinking, I can't go. I'm seventy-nine years old. But why not? What was stopping her now? From where Rose stood she could see the highway stretched out beyond the railroad. She'd been down that road before. Many times. But today it was calling for her.

"Don't worry, Gamma Rose," Annabeth said. "I'm old enough to drive."

A few knowing laughs came from the crowd.

"What's so funny?" Kyle asked Lily Bea.

Lily Bea wrapped her arm around Kyle's shoulders. "I'll tell you later. Better yet, read the book."

Annabeth took hold of Gamma Rose's hand. "I want to show you something." She guided Rose around to the back of the vehicle where the hatch was open.

Rose stared at the boxes of books. Those were *her* books filled with *her* words.

"Come on, Momma," Merle Henry said, opening the passenger door. "Go tell your stories."

The choice belonged to her now. Rose looked up at Annabeth. Then she studied the rest of her family, all three generations. She wanted to freeze this moment. She wanted to take each of them with her. But then Rose realized they would always be a part of her, just as she'd always be a part of them.

The tangerine sun was straight up in the sky. Rose could feel its warmth all the way through her bones. It seemed to be stirring things inside her. She didn't regret one minute of her life, but finally it was her turn.

Rose got inside the car and waved good-bye.

Acknowledgments

THE IDEA FOR these stories started with a picture I saw in *Down Cut Shin Creek: The Pack Horse Librarians of Kentucky* by Kathi Appelt and Jeanne Cannella Schmitzer. One photo revealed librarians working in a Louisiana bayou community. When I decided to write a generational book, I knew the stories would begin there. I owe a lot to Betty DeYeide Lockwood from Houma, who, at seventeen years old in the 1940s, drove the Terrebonne Parish Library Bookmobile. Her fabulous memory and her tireless energy contributed greatly to this book.

In addition to the above mentioned, I am also deeply grateful to the following: Mark Bahm with the Terrebonne Parish Library; Shannon Holt (many bouquets to you, my dear first reader); Jerry Holt; Christy Ottaviano—who convinced me this story was a novel, too; the Retreat Girls—Kathi Appelt, Lola Schaefer, Rebecca Kai Dotlich, and Jeanette Ingold—for that late-night writing exercise; Brenda Willis; Laurie and Tom Allen; the two Margarets— Margaret and Margaret Shaffer; Holly Alexander; the Amarillo Public Library (especially Pat Mullin and Carol Wallace); and the Rapides Parish Public Library.

About the Author

KIMBERLY WILLIS HOLT is the author of several award-winning novels, including *Keeper of the Night*; *When Zachary Beaver Came to Town*, which received the National Book Award for Young People's Literature; and *My Louisiana Sky*.

Seven generations of Ms. Holt's family were from Louisiana. Although Ms. Holt grew up in a military family and lived in many different places all over the world, Louisiana remained her emotional home. She now lives in west Texas with her family.

www.kimberlywillisholt.com

Go Fish!

GO FISH

KIMBERLY WILLIS HOLT

What did you want to be when you grew up?
A writer.

When did you realize you wanted to be a writer?
In seventh grade, three teachers encouraged my writing. That was when I first thought the dream could come true. Before that, I didn't think I could be a writer because I wasn't a great student and I read slowly.

What's your first childhood memory?
Buying an orange Dreamsicle from the ice-cream man. I was two years old.

What's your most embarrassing childhood memory?
In fourth grade, I tried to impress the popular girls that I wanted to be friends with by doing somersaults in front of them. (I never learned to do cartwheels.) They called me a showoff, so I guess it didn't work. If only I'd known how to do a cartwheel.

What was your worst subject in school?
Algebra.

What was your first job?
I was in the movies. I popped popcorn at the Westside Cinemas.

How did you celebrate publishing your first book?
I'm sure my family went out to dinner. We always celebrate by eating.

Where do you write your books?
I write several places—a soft, big chair in my bedroom, at a table on my screen porch, or at coffee shops.

Where do you find inspiration for your writing?
Most of the inspiration for my writing comes from moments in my childhood.

Which of your characters is most like you?
I'm a bit like most of them. However, I fashioned Tori in the Piper Reed books after me. But Tori is bossier than I was and she certainly makes better grades than I did.

When you finish a book, who reads it first?
My daughter listens to me read my first draft.

Are you a morning person or a night owl?
I'm a morning person.

What's your idea of the best meal ever?
That's a toss-up. My grandmother's chicken and dumplings, and sushi.

Which do you like better: cats or dogs?
I'm a dog person. I have a poodle named Bronte who is the model for Bruna in the Piper Reed series.

What do you value most in your friends?
Loyalty and honesty.

Where do you go for peace and quiet?
Home.

Who is your favorite fictional character?
Leroy in *Mister and Me* because he is forgiving. And that's a trait many of us don't have.

What are you most afraid of?
Anything harming my daughter.

What time of the year do you like best?
Fall.

What is your favorite TV show?
CBS Sunday Morning.

If you were stranded on a desert island, who would you want for company?
My husband and daughter.

What's the best advice you have ever received about writing?
A writer once told me, "Readers either see what they read or hear what they read. Writers have to learn to write for both." When I started following that advice, my writing improved.

What do you want readers to remember about your books?
The characters. I want them to seem like real people. I want them to miss them and wonder what happened to them.

What would you do if you ever stopped writing?
I plan on dying with a pen in my hand.

What do you like best about yourself?
I'm honest.

What is your worst habit?
I eat too much.

What do you consider to be your greatest accomplishment?
I gave birth to a wonderful human being.

What do you wish you could do better?
I wish I could do a cartwheel.

What would your readers be most surprised to learn about you?
I send gift cards with positive messages to myself when I order something for me.

*K*eep reading for an excerpt from
Kimberly Willis Holt's **The Dowser's Son**,
coming soon in hardcover from Henry Holt.

EXCERPT

Bittersweet Creek, 1833

Jake was known as the dowser. With a forked branch, he'd made his way from the Arkansas Territory to Missouri, stopping at farms to find water for new wells. His plan was to raise enough money so he could do what he wanted and never pick up the branch again. But the dowsing was a gift. And a gift might be abandoned, but it will always be there, waiting to be claimed.

One farmer didn't have money, so he paid Jake by giving him a parcel of land with a cabin. Since winter was settling in, Jake decided to stay there until spring, when he'd take up trapping. His cabin sat a hundred steps from Bittersweet Creek and about a mile, as the eagle flew, from the Hurd place. When their oldest daughter, Delilah, showed up at his door, begging for a place to stay, he'd not been with a woman in a long time. Without thinking, he said, "Well, I reckon I could marry you."

A few months later, Jake went west to trap. He left each fall and returned in the summer after the trappers' rendezvous. The life suited them. Delilah had a safe haven from her pa's temper, and Jake had someone to come home to. And most satisfying to them both were the months of solitude that they craved.

Delilah strolled through the woods, thinking about how that day felt especially hot. Jake would be making his way from Green Valley, and when he arrived he'd expect a clean house and a hot meal. She hurried home to prepare for him.

Anticipating Jake's arrival always brought on dread and excitement. Every year, Jake traded for supplies with an artist who painted the mountain man's way of life. Delilah looked forward to getting new paints, brushes, and paper. But she also loved her time alone in the woods. And the birds. She loved the birds.

Delilah treasured walking among the pines and cypress trees. She'd grown to appreciate the smell of her own sweat and the way it mixed with the musky smells of the earth. Now she'd have to wash all that away. Jake's return meant she'd have to bathe more often, keep house, and cook meals.

From him, she'd learned how appearances deceived. Her pa, Eb, was a small man who looked as gentle as a cat, while Jake was stocky, barrel-chested, and furry like a bear. He could talk until the sun fell out of the sky, but Jake didn't have a temper.

To Delilah, listening to Jake drone on and on about his trappings was a good trade-off.

A few days later, Jake arrived. He grabbed hold of Delilah and pressed his lips against hers. When it seemed he'd never let go, she wiggled free and grabbed the leather satchel in search of the new paints and brushes. She moved so quickly that the bag dropped with a *thump* to the floor, causing a glass to crack. Staring down at it, she could clearly see her own reflection. "What's that there?"

Jake sighed and collapsed upon a chair. "A mirr-o. Was one."

She took off his boots and fed him a bowl of vegetable and bacon soup. Jake gulped down the broth in less time than it took to sneeze. Then he fell asleep.

Delilah carefully set the hand mirror on the table next to her tablet and stared into it. The crack ran the entire length of the mirror, but what she saw fascinated her. She touched her red hair that frizzed like the threads on a ball of wool. When Delilah was a young girl, her ma braided it in a long pigtail and smoothed the wild hairs with lard. Delilah's finger stroked the lines of her nose and her wide chin. She smiled, not just because she was amused, but because she wanted to see what would happen to her face. She had a space next to her black tooth. She'd lost the tooth when Eb punched her for not milking the cow a few years back. Delilah was amazed that a piece of glass could reveal the history of her life. A fire burned inside her, and she began to draw.

In the middle of the night, Delilah heard Jake ease out of bed and pull on his boots. She knew what was next. He did it every summer when he returned. And she knew for sure he thought she didn't know. Last fall, she'd lifted the rock under the oak tree, hunting crickets for fish bait. She discovered the muslin sack buried in the ground under the rock. When she saw the money inside, she fell back on the ground and laughed. Jake didn't know her at all. Money didn't mean a thing in the world to Delilah.

For three months, Delilah cooked and cleaned for Jake, all the while gazing outside the window, praying for cool weather to come. Several weeks before the leaves turned crimson and orange, Jake packed up his mule and headed toward the mountains.

A month later, a sour taste formed in Delilah's mouth and she vomited her breakfast of bread and blackberry jam. Immediately she felt better, but the next morning, the sickness returned. Two months later, her belly began to round out like a melon. She cursed Jake's name to the trees, even threatening to kill him.

Then one November night, as if the heavens had heard her cries, light poured through the cabin window, awakening Delilah from her sleep. She hurried to the porch and discovered streaks of light streaming across the sky. All the stars are falling, thought Delilah. But instead of being afraid, she settled on the top step and watched. There were thousands, too many to count, and so she didn't even try. She just waited and watched. The light was so bright she could clearly see a doe and her young buck in the thick of the woods. The heavens had given her a gift. And hours later, when the shower of light ended, she felt sad.

The next day, Delilah awoke craving bread. Before sunset, she'd baked twelve loaves and eaten three. She tore the other loaves in tiny pieces and scattered them on the porch. In the morning, the birds had discovered her offering. She pushed the table next to the window and began to paint.

By the time winter arrived, Delilah's resentment had disappeared and a softness for the life inside her was growing. Though at times she believed they were in conflict with each other. When Delilah curled up in bed to sleep, the baby kicked, hard, until she got up and walked the floor. At which time the baby became still. Whenever Delilah settled at the table to draw, the baby caused a burning inside her gut that made her drop the pencil and give up for the day.

She began to dream the same vision each night. In her dreams, she heard a baby cry. Then she saw herself standing by a long winding river. A baby floated by, his little arms stretching toward her. But try as she did, she could not reach him. Downriver, a woman picked up the baby and handed him to another woman. That woman handed him to yet another. And so it went, the baby being passed down through a chain of women along the river. This dream occurred so often, Delilah started to think of it as a premonition. No matter what, she believed her child was destined for trials and tribulations. He would struggle. Delilah was certain of it.

Spring arrived, and Delilah spotted new nests every day. She discovered them in tree branches and corners under the porch cover. She even found one in the hole of the barn wall. The birds crafted their nests from bits of twigs, dead grass, corn husks, and Delilah's hair. She loved seeing her red strands woven in with all the other textures. She always believed she was a part of nature. This was proof of it.

In May, the baby birds began their flight lessons, and a feeling came over Delilah that she, too, was about to spread her wings and take off. She couldn't explain it, but the feeling became stronger each day.

One afternoon, as she walked through the woods, an old black bird called out to her. *A-mos*, it said. *A-mos, a-mos*. The wind began to howl, but she could still hear the bird's chant. *A-mos, a-mos, a-mos*.

When it was time for her baby, she had no choice but to fetch her ma. She set out for their cabin, walking the mile through the dense woods. Even though it was May, the mornings remained cold. And since there was no worn path, Delilah followed the smell of smoke rising from her parents' chimney. The pains in her womb kept her from noticing the cloud of birds flying above the treetops that towered over her head.

As she'd predicted, her brother Silas was hoeing the garden with Eb.

"I heard you coming the whole way," Eb said. "I could hear those dad-gum birds. They's always following you."

Eb feared birds ever since one swept down and pecked him in the nose. The incident happened three years ago after he'd taken a strike at Delilah. That was when she took off for Jake's cabin.

A huge flock of crows landed in the garden. Silas removed his hat and waved it overhead as he ran about trying to scare them away. His long thin limbs caused him to resemble a scarecrow that suddenly came to life. The birds flew away from Silas's reach, circled the garden, then returned.

"Shoo! Shoo!" Silas hollered as he flapped his hat, turning to his right, then his left. He started to spin.

If she'd not been in pain, Delilah would have laughed.

Eb narrowed his eyes at Delilah's stomach. "Looks like you got yourself in a heap of mess, gal."

"I had me a man to help."

Wiping his forehead with his sleeve, he said, "I can see that."

"Jake's my husband."

"I reckon you want your ma. Lolly's in the house." He turned away from her and joined Silas in his crusade, stomping his feet at a circle of crows.

Delilah felt the air close up around her. Just returning there had brought back all the bad thoughts. Then Daisy, her seven-year-old sister, ran over and hugged her legs. The tiny girl stared up at Delilah's big stomach and said, "You're as fat as an old grizzly bear."

Delilah stroked her sister's golden-red hair. "And you're as tiny as a little squirrel."

Her other siblings acted as if she were a stranger, cowering behind the ladder that led up to the loft. That bothered her most, more than seeing her pa. They've been poisoned against me, she thought. Or maybe they resented her for leaving because Eb had gone to hitting one of them. Her eyes searched each of their faces and arms for bruises, lingering longest on Daisy's. Relieved to discover none, Delilah figured she was probably the lone thorn in her pa's side.

Delilah wanted to return to her cabin for the baby to be born, but Lolly insisted on finishing Eb's dinner first. The pains came quicker, and Delilah paced on the front porch until Lolly finally joined her. They were making their way through the woods, heading back to the cabin, when Delilah's water broke. Before the sun was down, she was crying out for Jake.

The birds' chatter grew so loud that Lolly hollered, "Them birds are driving me crazy!"

The labor was long and hard, which puzzled Lolly since she'd merely grunted and pushed one time to bring each of her babies into the world. And when Lolly saw more blood coming from Delilah than she'd ever seen with all her own births put together, she suspected the outcome wouldn't be good.

Delilah's screams turned to groans, and her groans became whimpers.

Lolly went outside and found a stick, then gave it to Delilah. "Here, bite down on this."

Delilah yanked it from her mouth and slung it across the room. "It tastes like mud."

When the baby finally came, he was red as a ripe raspberry. Wails escaped from his wide mouth as he shook his tiny fists in the air.

Chuckling, Lolly held him up. "This boy is mad." She placed him next to Delilah's breast to suckle. "He's a strong one. What you reckon you'll call him?"

Delilah's lips brushed the light fuzz on his head, and she closed her eyes. Her words came out soft. "Amos is a good name."

"Amos?" Lolly mused. "Where in tarnation did you get that from?"

Delilah didn't answer. She just said, "Tell Jake I done my best. Don't let my baby forget me."

With that, she took her last breath. The cabin and the world outside the window grew silent. And every bird at Bittersweet Creek flew away.